Metropolitan Borough of Calderdale

Horrorscope

Horrorscope

Derek Lambert

PIATKUS

Copyright © 1993 by Derek Lambert

First published in Great Britain in 1993 by
Judy Piatkus (Publishers) Ltd of
5 Windmill Street, London W1P 1HF

**The moral right of the author
has been asserted**

*A catalogue record for this book is available
from the British Library*

ISBN 0-7499-0205-1

Phototypeset in 11/12pt Linotron Times by
Computerset, Harmondsworth, Middlesex
Printed and bound in Great Britain by
Biddles Ltd, Guildford and King's Lynn

Acknowledgement

My thanks to American figure painter Beryl Kranz who now lives in Spain. She guided my pen through the contours of her art. Any inelegant brush-strokes are mine not hers.

Thanks also to George and Pat Gilbert for their detective work.

Foreword

I began this book with an open mind about astrology. I neither believed nor disbelieved although, to be frank, I was inclined towards cynicism. When I started writing I consulted an astrologer, an attractive and delightful lady named Chris Horrigan who lives in St Albans in England and asked her to give me predictions for a fictitious heroine born at 5.30 a.m. on June 1st, 1962, in New Jersey. An exhaustive astro-analysis complete with chart calculated from the position of the planets at the moment of birth arrived when I was half way through the narrative. The horoscope anticipated for this woman who exists only in my mind so closely conformed to the inclinations and actions that I had already chronicled that some of my cynicism was dissipated. I still do not believe but my disbelief now wavers as irresolutely as the glimmer of the stars on a deep bright night.

'The fault, dear Brutus, is not in our stars,
But in ourselves, that we are underlings'
– William Shakespeare

'Or is it?' – Sarah Logan

Chapter One

You will be subject to attentions from a stranger . . .

Not so far.

She glanced at her wristwatch. 4.18 p.m. Outside the studio evening mist was gathering among the paper birch trees.

'Anything worrying you?' asked the naked woman on the couch.

'Doubt, I guess,' Sarah Logan said. 'I often get it at this late stage in a painting.'

'Maybe you should get another model.'

'No, you're just fine.'

Which she was. Lolling with weary decadence, belly spilling a little, eyes smudged. Voluptuous when transferred to the canvas. No box of chocolates, no wine . . . Instead Sarah had given her a telephone and placed her right hand on the receiver.

'. . . someone younger.'

'No, really, you're absolutely right.' You had to be diplomatic with amateur models like Janice Gotthardt who confused a canvas with a mirror. 'You know, I have to interpret, to exaggerate.'

You will be subject to attentions from a stranger . . .

By now – 4.35 – a prediction as incisive as that would normally have been fulfilled. Stupid. It's you who makes them come true. Isn't it?

'A lot of people take me for much younger.'

'I can believe that, truly.'

Sarah put down her brush and walked to the window, passing the collective scrutiny of a dozen nudes, sensuality and vulnerability perpetuated in acrylics. The evening was bladed with cruelty; departing sun isolated from its rays by the mist; forest stripping for deep winter.

She noticed a movement among the silver stems of the birches. A squirrel? A few leaves dropped, spinning, to the ground. She closed the drapes, intimately encompassing Janice Gotthardt and herself.

Janice's hand relaxed on the handle of the old-fashioned black telephone that Sarah had bought in a junk shop further south between Newburgh and Bear Mountain; her legs had opened a little, widening the apex of thick pubic hair. Sarah picked up her brush and gave more definition to the droop of one heavy breast. In trying to capture the susceptibility of such a woman one of the perils was imparting your own mood.

She clenched the brush between her teeth and stood back to assess the emotions of the woman materializing on the canvas.

What sort of attentions?

When she took the brush from her mouth she noticed that she had cut the lacquer on the handle with her teeth.

'How am I coming along?' Janice asked.

'Just fine.'

Maybe a box of chocolates wouldn't have been such a bad idea. A cliché only became one because it was apposite; by taking evasive action you sometimes lost realism.

Who did the woman want to call on the phone? A lover who no longer arrived on time? Husband, son . . .? What she wanted was reassurance, no question.

Who doesn't? Me, since Harry died?

'Why don't you pick up that phone?' she said to Janice.

'You painted me already with my hand resting on it.'

'If you were going to pick it up, who would you be calling?'

'Strictly confidential.'

'Pick it up,' Sarah said. *Because I want to see anticipation in the spider-webs at the corners of your eyes, at the tip of your cat's tongue* . . .

'You're the boss.'

She picked up the receiver and Sarah saw the skin on her forehead tighten.

'Okay,' Sarah said. 'That's fine, great.'
'So who was I calling?'
'Someone who matters.'

Sarah changed paints and brush to snare what-might-have-been on the face on the canvas. Supposing the antique phone which wasn't connected suddenly rang . . . She wiped spots of paint from her jeans and sweater.

'I'm getting kind of restless,' Janice said. 'You know how it is at night when you want to change from your left side to your right?'

'And you wish you had a third side? Sure, I know. Okay, let's take a break. Coffee?' She stuck masking tape on the outlines of the pose.

'Got anything a little stronger?'

'Wine?'

'Wine would be fine. I don't drink that much but every so often . . .' She sat upright, thighs fleshed out against the edge of the couch, and gulped Californian red.

Sarah looked through the skylight above the big, paint-splodged easel that reminded her of an instrument of torture from the Inquisition. She liked it when her gaze was returned by the stars but tonight darkness was pressed against the glass by the mist.

She wandered round the studio which was a tip. But you got away with untidiness if you were an artist. Especially if you were also a widow.

She stopped in front of a self-portrait, a nude, a failure. Lifelike enough – long limbs, good, centre-fold breasts, chestnut hair in plaited pigtail, even the appendectomy scar – but not arousing any curiosity. Perhaps because the artist knew the model too well.

'Mind if I ask you a question?' Janice said.

'Shoot.' She knew what the question would be.

'Why do you, a woman, paint nudes?' She examined her empty glass as though it might contain the answer and Sarah refilled it.

How about killing her with this: 'Rather than have the model as either an "action photograph" or in "frozen immobility" I have tried to create an independent existence as design, retaining the human quality and the pose fully expressed by accentuating what is characteristic in the model. The painting itself should appear fresh and spontaneous. As Balthus once said, "I am always eager not to tire the canvas."' From her thesis for a Master of Fine Arts degree at the Pratt Institute in Brooklyn. Room 106, Higgins Hall.

That would certainly freeze Janice Gotthardt into immobility. Instead she recited: 'Because I want to paint life and life begins in a woman's body. Fertility, procreation, sex . . .'

Now the back-up question, you could bet on it.

'Yeah, but why not nude men?'

'Because I don't like painting dicks,' Sarah Logan said.

Janice spilled wine between her breasts.

Sarah said: 'Mind if I ask you a question?'

'Go ahead.' She brushed ineffectually at the rivulet of wine with the tips of her plump fingers.

'Do you follow the stars?'

'Sure I do. Every morning in the newspaper. I'm Libra. Lazy Libra.' She smiled nervously.

'So you weigh up people, huh? The scales, the only inanimate sign of the Zodiac. And you're smart and capable of balanced judgement, right?'

'Not so dumb anyway. Why?'

'I guess I was seeking . . . reassurance.'

'I don't understand.'

That I'm not a freak, Sarah thought.

She said: 'Okay, let's get back to work. There, lie back, relax, hand on the phone, remember that call you want to make.'

Sarah added cadmium red light and yellow light to a blob of titanium white for flesh. The wine between Janice's breasts was evocative but she resisted painting it. She worked instead on the raised hip.

'What's your sign?' Janice asked.

'Gemini. The Twins.'

'You really believe all that stuff?'

'I don't believe or disbelieve.'

'I read somewhere that Marlene Dietrich wouldn't move until she had read her horoscope – poor woman.'

And Aristotle. And Isaac Newton, Milton, Byron, Napoleon . . .

'And Nancy Reagan,' Janice said. 'So that must have included Ronald Reagan when he was president. Can you imagine, all that power in the hands of a star-gazer?'

If I'm going to be subject to *attentions from a stranger*, Sarah thought, it won't be here in this studio. 'Okay, let's call it a day,' she said, and began to fidget around the studio, indicating, she hoped, that she was anxious to leave.

'I can give it another half hour. That was the time we agreed.'

'I'll pay whatever we agreed.'

'That wasn't –'

'I know, I'm sorry. You're a terrific model, Janice.'

'I thought maybe we were collaborating, sharing . . .'

'We are,' Sarah said. 'Believe me, we are.'

'Sometimes I feel more like her –' pointing at the canvas – 'than I do myself.'

'That's good! That means I've captured *you*,' Sarah lied.

'Vic gets a bit jealous.'

'It happens,' Sarah said. 'Because you're the centre of the sort of attention he can never command.' She dropped her brushes into Maxwell House coffee cans, each containing water, and sniffed the clouding fluid, the smell reminding her of a childhood classroom.

'He does okay,' Janice said of her husband, who drove truck-loads of timber and occasionally beat her up. 'He doesn't need attention.'

'He's a good man,' Sarah said.

'Not that good.' Janice helped herself to more wine and began to dress.

A breeze had awakened from the direction of the Catskills; hopefully it was blowing the mist back to the Hudson. Sarah looked again for stars through the sky-light but saw only squares of darkness.

'A guy once told me that a half-dressed woman was more sexy than one in the buff,' Janice said. 'He reckoned a stripper should start her act naked and then get dressed slowly and stop when she was, you know, halfway there. But he was kind of weird.' She struggled into a black leather skirt.

'He was right, of course.'

'Maybe you can do a painting of me like that. A present for Vic. Gift-wrapped.' She laughed throatily, fighting her way into a moulting fur jacket, finding her shoes with her feet. Dressing for Janice Gotthardt was a work-out. 'Gotta rush. Vic'll be back soon and he's been on the road for two days.'

She hurried out of the studio banging the door behind her. Her footsteps clattered up the brick path beside the butterfly house and died in the mist. The cough of her rusty green Dodge reached Sarah faintly and she wondered why Janice was suddenly in such a hurry when a few minutes earlier she had been happy to 'give it another half hour'.

She tidied up. Nothing drastic: put the rest of the brushes out to graze, screwed the caps on the tubes of acrylic. The ooze of paint always made her salivate.

The wind got up a little more and played flaky music in the shingled walls of the house across the disgraceful lawn. A hot bath, a Martini, dinner at the Silver Springs, early to bed, warm dreams in which Harry might beckon . . . A beautiful place, bed, as you get older.

She stretched her arms above her head, felt her sweater move with her body, looked through the sky-light. And screamed.

Chapter Two

. . . but you will find comfort from an unexpected source.

The village – or town, it depended on your civic pretensions – was named Holyfield because there was an Indian burial ground on the outskirts close to Sarah Logan's house. It was situated to the west of Route 9W in upstate New York but there was enough hill and forest in between to swallow the noise of the traffic, most of which dropped into the valley of the Hudson to the east.

Holyfield was, in fact, insular. The sawmill kept its workforce from wasting south to New York city; its history, studiously preserved by its womenfolk, encouraged casual tourists but repelled encroachment. Trapped within its amber was a library with an Indian section devoted to the Iroquois and lacrosse – ORIGINALLY AN AMERICAN NATIVE GAME, in case you didn't know – in which lonely men hid from the cold. A grocery store that smelled of soap flakes and mice. A church kneeling in the square. Griswold's drugstore, the offices of the *Holyfield Banner*, Noveck's soda fountain and a long dark bar where customers sat, nursing glasses between knitted fingers.

The buildings in the centre were clap-board or weathered stone. Noble mansions lay to the west on the fringes of Silver Lake, which also boasted the Silver Springs restaurant and a country club. The sawmill was situated a decent distance to the east, where the community was poorer – sagging automobiles pinned outside houses like discarded brooches – and was visited by neither tourists nor citizens of the town itself.

The seclusion of Holyfield proper attracted a few students of esoteric interests, among them a grey-haired black professor named Ambrose Moon, who was compiling the definitive book on the language of gestures, and a white woman from Albany writing a thesis on rape victims. The isolation had in the past also encouraged a measure of incest that accounted for the occasional smile of beautific innocence before its owner committed an act of indecency. Such acts were largely ignored unless the offender became too precocious, in which case he was taken away by businesslike nurses, usually at night.

But, by and large, Holyfield was an orderly haven: a condition that state trooper, Sam Parker, a lean and healthy-skinned jogger, strove to perpetuate. And it was towards his office behind the church that Sarah Logan drove to report what she had seen in the sky-light.

But did she really want to report it to Parker?

At first, naturally: scream dying in her throat, foot hard on the gas pedal of her BMW. But what *had* she seen? A face at a window? Parker would indulge her politely, finger sawing the cleft in his chin, before consigning her statement to the IBM under *Unsubstantiated* – or, worse, *Neurotic*. She braked, tyres skidding on errant gravel on the paved road leading from her house into Holyfield. No, to hell with that. Shit, an intruder *had* been spying. From the roof of the studio. She had seen his forehead bone-white against the glass, his teeth sharp. Whether or not Parker believed her, he should be told in case worse followed. She put her foot down again.

Lights glowed cosily in houses as children settled in front of TV to await the return of the breadwinner. She saw women closing drapes, pulling down shutters, blinding the windows to the desolate night.

Forehead, teeth and, yes, eyes . . . But had she truly seen them or had they merely been the *attentions from a stranger* anticipated too intensely? For a long time after Harry's death she had observed phenomena that had proved to be illusory.

Had the light from the studio fashioned the face in the mist? She peered through the windshield. Where was the mist? Just a few feathers of it lying low among the trees where the

Indians were buried. Determination flagging, she drove into Holyfield at a reflective speed. *But you will find comfort from an unexpected source.*

She stopped the BMW in the square which was deserted except for a back-packer with a maple leaf on his rucksack who had lost Canada. She drummed her fingers on the steering wheel. Sam Parker was just round the corner. But Sam figured that women who lived alone were courting trouble – and in that he wasn't alone.

She engaged DRIVE and drove to Pacey's where, in Parker's view, women alone were also asking for something. Inside, she ordered a Beefeater gin and tonic and glanced at the nearest figure hunched in the twilight in silent communion with his drink.

'Ben Deacon,' she said, 'what the hell are you doing here?'

Driving to New York from Albany where he had a patient, her one-time psychotherapist told her; so he had crossed the Hudson at Poughkeepsie and called her from there; but she hadn't replied. He had stopped anyway, just in case.

'I was at home.' She wanted to touch his questing nose and the soft skin under his eyes. But he had told her long ago that such inclinations were merely the manifestations of a patient seeking reassurance. Shrinks should never get involved with patients was what he had been saying and she had accepted that.

'All day,' she said. 'And I've got two numbers. One in the house, one in the studio, the way Harry wanted it.'

'I called them both,' Ben said in between sips of his drink – bourbon if she remembered correctly. 'One rang, one was dead.'

'Which?'

'Which was dead? The one in your studio.'

'What time did you call?'

'Quarter after four.'

'I got a call just before that. From the gallery.'

'So it went kaput immediately after that.'

'I guess so.' She swirled her drink and listening to the wind-chime tinkle of the ice.

'You look as though –'

'I've seen a ghost. Maybe I have.'

Sam Parker, immaculate in his grey uniform and stetson, came in. He nodded at Sarah. No more than he expected, his expression said, and she realized she was still wearing her paint-splattered clothes. Finding no outward evidence of delinquency Parker returned to the great adventure that was the outdoors.

'I think we'd better have dinner and talk about it,' Deacon said. 'You were going to the Silver Springs, weren't you?'

'How did you know?'

'You look hungry,' he said obliquely.

'I can't go like this,' smoothing her hands down her heather-coloured sweater.

'The Silver Springs isn't the Lutèce, for Christ's sake!'

But they *were* particular, and the head waiter hustled them to an alcove the way police sometimes bundle criminals out of a courthouse. And their order – rack of lamb broiled with thyme – was taken promptly in the hope that they would be gone by the time guests from the noble mansions arrived.

Sarah began to relax. The restaurant with its crackling log fire reminded her of Chez Henri in Sugarbush. A plagiarism, because the Vermont bistro owned by Henri Borel, former food controller for Air France, had been there first.

Deacon snapped his fingers as though he was startling a patient out of a trance and a waiter materialized, averting his gaze from the sweater. Deacon ordered a bottle of Beaujolais-Lantignié.

While they were waiting he asked her whether she still based her daily life around her astrological predictions, a practice that he had warned her about when she had first consulted him in Manhattan. 'A dependency not sufficiently recognized in my business.' Well, sure – and what about all the millions of other rational citizens who consulted the stars, not to mention the untold numbers of orientals who were guided by *T'ung Shu*, the ancient Chinese almanac?

'Astrology can be dangerous,' Deacon made a performance of tasting the wine to put the waiter in his place, 'because it takes away your God-given initiative. You are manipulated.'

'You're over-simplifying. It's the angles of the sun and the planets at the time of your birth that affect you.'

Why not? The theory had as much going for it as any other. More, when you stared into a starlit sky glimmering with secrets that astronomers had never solved, merely tagged with terrestrial interpretations. Black holes indeed!

'All an astrologer does,' Sarah said, 'is deduce how the movements of the planets and their relationship with the earth influence you.'

'But you adapt to their prophecies: your life isn't your own anymore.'

'Wrong.' She was surprised at her vehemence. 'What they foretell is what was going to happen anyway. The astrologer gives you the means to cope with it.'

Deacon sighed theatrically. 'So you're still hooked?'

'Does it surprise you?'

'No, I guess not,' he said as the lamb arrived.

A winter day aching with cold. Ice creaking on the lake, frost in woodland hollows, pewter sky threatening snow. Not even Harris could be persuaded to go snouting for rabbits with his mongrel nose.

It was a Monday, and over breakfast in the stripped pine kitchen she opened the second of the week's predictions which in those days arrived by mail, seven envelopes in a master package posted in Manhattan.

An unruly time for your emotions. Your ruler, Mercury, is falling back and in the first half of the day you will suffer a disappointment because a meeting with someone close to you will be cancelled.

Harry finished buttering a slice of toast and bit into it incisively. 'I forgot to tell you last night,' he said. 'I can't make it for lunch. Got a meeting with –'

'And you knock astrology?'

'Pardon me?'

'It doesn't matter,' she said, watching the busy movement of his jaw as he chewed toast. For an owner of an art gallery – part-owner, that was – he was almost too positive. In the public eye anyway. But that's what you needed when you were dealing with artists. Me for sure, she thought, and smiled at him forgivingly, grateful to Manet, Matisse and Piero della Francesca for bringing them together. Not to mention Fragonard.

Partners may have worries that you do not comprehend, so make allowances for the unknown. Aggravation might exacerbate the situation.

She waited for him to tell her about his worries; instead he poured himself more coffee, picked up the *New York Times* and read it through the steam.

'You're not worried about anything are you, Harry?' she asked, addressing the *Times*.

'Not unless you know something I don't.'

But there *was* something. She could sense it. Or was she affected by the forecast?

'We should always share.' She felt unable to leave it alone.

'How can I share nothing?'

'Why don't you give New York a miss today?'

'Miss a meeting with Robert Hughes? Are you crazy? And it's your paintings we're hanging.'

'Nudes in this weather.' Sarah shivered and Harris laid his black and white clown's face on her knee.

Prepare yourself for a loss in the family.

Her mother in Fort Lauderdale? She hadn't been well.

'Please, Harry. Don't drive into New York.'

He put down the newspaper with exaggerated deliberation and she noticed on his face the stamp of fatigue that had survived sleep: the face of an artist who, accepting his lack of talent, had become an executive.

'I have to go, and please don't try and think for me.' He pressed his eyes with the tips of his fingers. 'What is it, anyway – something in your horoscope?'

'Why tempt fate?'

'Crazy,' he said. 'Just crazy.' He spanned his forehead with thumb and forefinger, pressing the temples, investing them with eggshell fragility.

'There's no harm in it. Ten million people in the States follow the stars. More than four thousand astrologers. It gives people . . . direction.'

'You need direction?'

'Not since I found you, I guess.'

'So why –'

'I'll cancel the horoscopes,' she spread honey on a finger of toast and Harris drooled, 'if you stay here today.'

'Jesus Christ! I'm going to New York for *us*, don't you understand that?'

'If it's for us, don't go.'

He fetched his black Crombie, the hat with the broad and slightly theatrical brim that was a concession to lost aspirations, driving gloves and grey granny scarf. She waited for him at the door, hugging her sensible robe around her. 'Anyway, drive carefully,' she said, still hoping he would relent.

He paused, took off one leather glove, held her chin between his fingers and kissed her dry lips, arousing the jealousy of Harris who placed his paws on his chest, then hers. 'Sorry I snapped,' he said. 'You know how it is.'

Sarah, who didn't, said: 'You still don't –'

'Martinis. Six o'clock on the button. Then maybe a little decadence, Harris permitting.'

He opened the door and the cold hurried into the house. As he crossed the frosty and dishevelled lawn, weighted a little to one side by his briefcase, she called out to him but her voice froze in her throat.

That was the last time she saw him alive.

'Small wonder I'm still hooked,' she said to Deacon.

'It was a coincidence. They happen every day of our lives and yet they still surprise us. You're reading a book about cats and next day a stray comes meowing into your life. It would still have come if you'd been reading a book about the Yeti.'

'For a psychotherapist you're very down to earth.'

'That's what we have to do, Sarah – bring people down to earth. Teach them that there's no such thing as heavenly influences, unless you count God.'

'Then how do you explain what happened three months later?'

Winter melting, dormant life stirring, whispers in the forest, music of running water . . .

And still she heard his key in the lock. 'Left my spectacles behind, I'm going senile.'

'Trying to catch me with my lover, more like!'

A familiar joke, part of the routine of sharing that went unsung until you had no one to share it with. A routine that had begun immediately, in the Fragonard Room of the Frick with its paintings about love, in particular the four panels commissioned by Madame du Barry – *Love Letters, Pursuit, The Meeting* and *Lover Crowned*.

'At this stage we can dispense with the first panel.'

She had swung round and seen a young man in his mid-twenties – with a beard even in those days – his face with its flattish nose and brown eyes set in clasps of contradiction.

'We can?'

'*Lover Crowned* comes later.'

'How much later?'

'After *Pursuit*.'

'You're very fresh.' Disappointed by the choice of phrase, circa 1940, but laughing just the same and establishing what they later agreed was one of the two prerequisites of marriage – mutually triggered humour and good sex.

Later on a row boat on the mossy waters of the lake in Central Park, wondering why she had succumbed to such an outrageous pick-up, she tried to analyze the contradictions of his character. Aspirations thwarted by abilities? Cynically poised to accept the lot of 75 per cent of the populace who suffered an occupation rather than a calling? But for a frustrated artist with some money – 'Perhaps that's my handicap, I never starved in a garret' – there was a compromise. An art gallery. In SoHo. 'You paint, of course,' he said, digging the oars into the water, jostling with coins of late autumn sunlight.

'No,' she said, 'I canvas Peter Stuyvesant cigarettes. And yes,' trailing her fingers in the water, 'I paint as well.'

'Landscapes?'

'Nudes,' observing the quickening of interest with which she was already familiar in other men.

Over hamburgers in Jackson's Hole she rationed her CV item by item. Brooklyn College. Tendencies to artistic interpretation resented by her parents – now in retirement in Florida – but majoring nevertheless in art at Adelphi University, Garden City, Long Island.

'And then?'

'What about you?'

'Much the same. In Philadelphia. Except that I flunked.'

'Justified?'

'I guess so.'

'Honesty. I like that,' observing the rueful squeezing at the corners of his brown eyes. 'I went to Pratt where I got my MFA.'

'Can I see your . . . nudes?'

'Why not, provided they don't inflame you?'

'If they do?'

'Sometimes their bellies sag,' she said, spooning mint ice-cream with chocolate chips. 'Breasts too. Autumn can be more beautiful than spring,' she said. 'It's learned a lot.'

'I understand.'

So she showed him her nudes in her shared apartment in Brooklyn and he hung them in his gallery and sold one to an antique dealer, a voyeur who superimposed a photograph of his wife's face above the voluptuously autumnal body.

They made love two days after they met – *Lover Crowned*. He proposed on Christmas Day and they were married six months later with the approval of his parents, who subscribed to several worthy causes in Philadelphia, City of Brotherly Love, and hers, who journeyed north from the Sunshine State with dutiful resignation.

Five years of partnership – looking into the night sky and seeing the same star, being apart but together in a crowd – until the morning when she was advised that aggravation might *exacerbate the situation*.

What situation?

Had she been responsible for his disappearance?

For three months she hibernated in the house at Holyfield while the police made desultory attempts to trace Harry, implying that he wouldn't be the first husband in the State of New York to escape from a kook wife – 'kook' emerging as one of officer Sam Parker's favourite words.

'Kook because I paint naked women?'

A shrug of his lean shoulders, eyebrows reaching to his cap of cropped black hair as thick as fur. 'Maybe he took a fancy to one of them.'

'Then there's hope for him.'

'Whatever you say, ma'am,' eyebrows pushing at each other in incomprehension.

'Find him, officer.'
'We're doing everything –'
'Find him!'

Hibernating. Until one morning, watched by Harris, she read the latest prediction from the astrologer – *A long lost member of the family could return* . . .

The cup of coffee didn't actually fall from her hands. She didn't snap the toast between her fingers. Instead she reread the horoscope, salient point cossetted by three paragraphs of mundane prophecy.*Could return.*

She waited for the key in the lock.

An icicle dripped outside the window.

By midday, nothing.

She called Deacon and Harry's partner at the gallery, Mike Kaplan.

Nothing.

By mid-afternoon the more mundane aspects of the forecast had come true. The drip of the icicle re-froze. Pulled by an exuberantly snouting Harris, wearing a moulter beaver jacket and black boots over her jeans, Sarah made her way through the sparse fringe of birch, through alder and pine to the still-frozen lake on which, hand in hand, she and Harry had once walked until the ice began to split in fizzing cracks.

She stood on a spur beside a leaning alder. On the far side, maybe three-quarters of a mile away, pencil-point pines gave way to maple which, in the fall, glowed as extravagantly as any in Vermont. In summer you could boat and swim and fish, but in winter it was a lonely place because a child had once fallen through thin ice and drowned and skating was now forbidden. Which didn't stop teenagers from walking across it for bets. Today the ice had lost its density. Staring down from the spur Sarah imagined she could see fish flicking the surface of the water beneath it; to the right beside a wooden jetty a small area was still opaque.Frowning, she slid down the bank of the spur, pulling Harris behind her, walked along the slippery boards and peered down. From beneath the ice a face peered back.

'Some coincidence,' Sarah said. Deacon shrugged and asked the waiter for the check.

'And today that face in the sky-light . . . just the same but the other way up.' No, not quite the same – because what was left of Harry's face had been bloated and bloodless, the rest eaten by eels. She squeezed her eyes shut, opened them and finished her wine with a boozer's swallow.

'I'll stay at your house tonight,' Deacon said.

'Therapy stopped six months ago.'

'I'll stay just the same.'

'What about the shrink-patient syndrome?'

Deacon, she believed, harboured for her a quality known by other men as love; but not by a psychotherapist who dissected all messages from within the cranium and despised all generalities of the emotions. And, more than any physician, backed away from relationships with female patients because he had trespassed in areas of the psyche where no partner had any right to intrude.

'Don't worry, I'll sleep on the couch.'

'I might paint you.'

'I'll try to keep my mouth shut.'

'No,' she said as he picked up his credit card, 'I'll see this through myself. I have to, otherwise your treatment' – another word he rejected – 'will have been meaningless. So what's one Peeping Tom anyway? They're notorious cowards.'

'Are they?' Deacon said. 'I hadn't heard. I'll follow you back to the house just the same.'

On their way out of the restaurant they passed two sawmill executives and their wives settling hungrily at a table. The men glanced speculatively at Sarah but the women fielded the glances and they sank without a trace behind their menus. Sarah, followed by Deacon in his Cadillac, drove home slowly. The breeze had finally swept away the mist but the night was dark, stars peeping from occasional panes of clarity in the clouds. The gable of the house and the single tall chimney were just visible and the lights she had left burning in the kitchen and living-room reached the lawn and shrubbery, shining more brightly on the glass walls of the hothouse containing the butterflies.

There was no response from Harris, but he was always slow on the draw.

'Coffee?'

'No thanks,' Deacon said. 'Not if I'm not staying. But I'll stick around for a few minutes.'

'In case the peeper's still here?' She shook her head too emphatically. 'No chance. He probably came to drool over the model.' *So why was he still there after she had left?*

She opened the door and Harris loved them, tail swiping frantically.

'Mind if I look around?'

'Go ahead. I'll make coffee anyway.'

'All clear,' he said when he returned to the kitchen. 'So I'll be on my way. Why don't we meet next time you drive into Manhattan?'

'Monday,' she said. 'Week today, no problem. The Russian Tea Room. My treat.'

'Are you sure you're okay?'

'As okay as I'll ever be.' She played with one of Harris's ridiculous ears.

Listening to the roar and fade of the Cadillac, she picked up a flashlight and, accompanied by Harris, made her way across the lawn to the studio.

The beam picked out the door, the lock. She inserted her key. The beam found breasts, thighs, coyly turned shoulders, pubic thatches, daunting and disillusioned eyes that seemed to dilate in the inquisitive glare.

She prodded the beam at the skylight. Saw it stretching into the night where it was finally consumed.

Back in the kitchen she drank some of her coffee which had cooled and poured the balance down the sink. Then she climbed the stairs purposefully, ignoring the creak that had always been there under pressure.

Washed and stripped, but only down to bra and panties – why, she wasn't sure – she burrowed beneath the duvet in the sighing bed that had added its rhythmic protests to their love-making. One day, they had said, they would get the bed fixed. But they had always forgotten in the contented fatigue that ensued. Forgotten the creaking stair too.

The stair creaked in the early doze of her sleep.

Harris?

She went to the door of the bedroom, opened an acute angle and looked on to the landing. Harris swished his tail.

'Go to bed,' she said, returning to her own. The stair creaked as he made his way downstairs.

An hour or so passed. Faces peered into half-formulated dreams. Swashbuckling decisions – *going to stay here, and fuck you, whoever you are* – were followed by snatches of indecision.

She made herself breathe deeply and regularly. Heard Harris howl a few times: a wolf-like mating call that he had never emitted before. The howls followed her as she deep-breathed herself into slumbrous depths that only Deacon could comprehend.

Chapter Three

... You will encounter strong opposition to your ideals but, being a Geminian, you will negotiate these difficulties with flair. But do not rely too heavily on that other characteristic of yours, charm.

Friday.
    After breakfast she attended to the butterflies and moths, or *papillons de nuit* as the French more imginatively called them. Checked the humidifiers and the thermometers – 85 per cent humidity, 28 degrees C. Lingered in the tropical capsule on the frosted lawn while gossamer wings fluttered around her, each so exquisitely patterned that you could weep for the brevity of their lives: fifteen days, no longer.
    It was the transience of their beauty that had first attracted Sarah to lepidoptera on their honeymoon in France when they visited *Le Jardin des Papillons* at Rocamadour. From egg to caterpillar to chrysalis – so much fertile endeavour for a fortnight of fragile life and courtship.
    Harry had bought her the hot-house when they returned from their honeymoon and stocked it from a dealer near Pearl Paint on Canal Street where she bought her acrylics.
    In mixing paints she tried to find the colours of their wings – the azure of a Ulysses from Australia, the scarlet splashes of *Papilo rumanzovia* from the Phillipines – and always managed to finish a picture within two weeks. If you looked very carefully you could always find a butterfly in one of Sarah Logan's paintings: in a drape or a shawl or a fragment of chiffon. Finding one, pundits often commented that Whistler had signed his paintings with a butterfly.

What confounded her were the butterflies whose colours changed when viewed from different angles, *Troides magellanus*, for instance, whose lower wing changed from yellow to sky blue. The giant *Attacus atlas* moth also defeated her – hatched without a proboscis with which to imbibe nectar, it lived for only a week and she couldn't equal that in a painting.

A green Birdwing from New Guinea, four black spots on each of the lower wings, flitted past her face and landed on a mauve bouganvillaea. She looked for *Attacus atlas* and found it perched on a heliotrope plant, big brown wings folded, smudged pink eyes at the tips of its upper wings hidden. 'Wake up,' she said. 'With only a week to live you can't afford to sleep.' The wings quivered. Shaking her head, she let herself out of the tropics into North America in mid-winter, coughing as razored air reached her lungs.

Back in the house she called Janice Gotthardt to tell her she wouldn't be wanting her today. Her husband answered. Dear old hard-knuckled Vic. Sarah had never met him but she imagined he made a habit of hoisting a beer belly with his hands and belching. Surprisingly he had a small voice.

'Yeah, Sarah –' the immediate first-name familiarity irritated her – 'how you doing?'

Sarah said she was doing okay. 'But I won't be needing Janice today.'

'Won't be needing her? *Needing*, I like that. What do *you* need, Sarah?'

Slobs like you, I don't. Was he even now trying to stuff his gut beneath his belt? 'I'll pay for her time, of course.'

'Of course. You and me must get together some time. You know, we both know Janice . . . intimately.'

'She's a great model.'

'Maybe I could watch some day while you paint her.'

'I don't think so, Mr Gotthardt. Very private, the relationship between artist and model.'

'That's what I figured.'

'Is that supposed to mean anything?'

'Nothing you could take offence about, Sarah.'

'Tell her next Tuesday when I get back from New York.'

'She'll be there as God made her.'

'How did God make you, Mr Gotthardt?'

She cradled the receiver. Surely that wasn't the *strong opposition* to her ideals?

She walked across the lawn, pot-holed by Harris, and from the drawer of a paint-daubed desk in the studio took out the original correspondence with the astrologer Athena, warrior goddess of wisdom, patron of the arts, and a virgin: in reality a feisty blonde occupying a penthouse on the East Side of midtown Manhattan with dreamy, short-sighted blue eyes and a ten-year-old son.

I am delighted you have decided to put your trust in the planets. As you probably know many forecasts are based purely on the position of the sun in relation to your planet and will indicate tendencies for a particular day.

However, to achieve total accuracy I need to know your place of birth – precise longitude and latitude if possible, but approximate will do – and the time you were born, preferably to the nearest hour or minute even.

(Date of birth, June 1st, 1962. Place, a beach resort in New Jersey. Time 5.30 a.m.)

Leave me to calculate GMT and sidereal time, i.e. time based on the rotation of the earth in relation to a particular star. Confused? You needn't be. I am merely trying to make the point to you that astrology is a science and not a popular indulgence.

Your natal horoscope is calculated from the position of the planets when you were born. It is, with the exception of Siamese twins, unique to an individual, because no one is born at precisely the same time and location as anyone else.

If you are sceptical, do not forget that it is an established fact that celestial phenomenon do affect events on earth: sun spots, comets and moon phases, for instance.

Subsequent predictions, after your birth chart has been mapped, depend on the movements of the planets in relation to that chart. But do not forget that those predictions must always be considered in the context of the chart, i.e. if danger is in the offing it would be more perilous to a subject whose chart indicates a headstrong personality . . . But your destiny is always in your own hands.

Did Athena protest too much?

The predictions had maintained a casual accuracy until the day Harry had disappeared; until the day the half-devoured face had stared at her from a window of ice. Even now she saw the eel peering from an eye socket.

An astrological chart had followed. She studied its geometric detail. Time, date and place of birth recorded in the centre: spokes emanating from the core dividing a fixed inner circle into twelve segments known as houses, each representing an aspect of life – personality, health and death – an outer wheel split among the twelve signs of the Zodiac from Aries the Ram (swashbuckling and dominant) to Pisces (emotional, of kindly disposition.) The outer wheel had been rotated so that in the smaller, fixed circle, the position of the planets plus the sun and moon at her moment of birth had been established.

The ruling planet for a Gemini was Mercury, characterized by an ability to communicate. *Is that why I'm an artist?* In the heavens it was the smallest and fastest planet, closest to the Sun.

There were other factors in the birth chart but the essence of it was the relationship of the Zodiacal signs, houses and planets.

Did she truly believe? Well, astrology was at least four thousand years old and many great men of diverse intellects had supposedly believed.

She began to read the interpretations of the chart. *The position of the sun indicates that you are intellectual, communicative, sociable, reluctant to display emotion.* Unless I see a face staring at me through a skylight.

Your rising sign, Pisces – the part of the Zodiac that was due east of your birthplace at the time you were born – implies that you feel deeply, display a mysterious air and can feel other people's pain or joy.

Other phenomena showed that she was *sensual and possessive about people close to her, generous but careful in small matters.*

The rising planet Jupiter indicated *an attraction to the darker side of life* and suggested that *strange occurrences might beset your partner.*

Sarah shivered.

She often experienced the worst side of other people's characters . . . she possessed a *rebellious streak* . . . the position of Uranus, the Great Awakener, *demonstrates a desire to shock* . . .

Like painting nudes within a prudish society?

Uranus, she read, ruled the twelfth house – the last segment of the circular framework of the chart. With Pisces rising and Jupiter in the ascendant it ruled dreams, fantasies and mysticism. It also related to *unseen enemies*.

Again she shivered.

But Saturn came to her rescue in the twelfth. *It protects you, gives you a practical streak and provides you with loyal friends, although you may not realise who these friends are because they are outside your artistic circle.*

You feel the flow of life . . .

In my paint brush?

Gauguin had been a Gemini. So had Marilyn Monroe and John F. Kennedy.

For a Gemini woman the answer to her romantic prayers was a Leo, sign of love. A Leo swept you off your feet. Harry had been a Leo. 'At this stage we can dispense with the first . . .' *Love Letters*, that was.

Later she called Sam Parker because the glimpse of the face in the sky-light, imaginary or otherwise, had been followed by the lupine howling of Harris for four consecutive nights.

Parker was unexpectedly cooperative. 'I'll be round within the hour, Mrs Logan.'

'Is that necessary?' Stupid, but somehow she hadn't anticipated Parker prowling around the house, the garden, the butterfly house, the studio. 'I'm reporting a prowler, is all.'

'Is this a serious report, Mrs Logan?'

'Yes, but –'

'Then, sure as hell, I've got to come round.'

She put on her working clothes, heather sweater and tacky jeans, and combed her hair primly.

He arrived in civilian clothes, tweed jacket with leather elbows.

'So what have we got here?' he said, accepting a can of beer in the kitchen where she seemed to live these days.

'What we have,' she said, matching him with a beer, 'is a sighting.'

'Description?'

He looked as though he wanted to plant his feet, legs crossed, on the kitchen table but had, at the last moment, desisted. It never ceased to amaze her how men's attitudes changed in the presence of a divorced or widowed woman.

'Just a face. Through a sky-light.'

'Like the face under the ice? I always meant to apologize about that – you know, suggesting that maybe your husband hadn't really disappeared.'

'Yeah, well, no one ever quite explained what he was doing under the ice, did they?'

'Right.' He sawed at the cleft in his chin. 'The sheriff's office reckoned –'

'It was suicide.'

'With respect, everything pointed that way. He'd been in the water for maybe three months and the ice must have been thin when he went in. He knew how goddam' treacherous it was. Didn't you once –'

'Walk on the ice together? Yes, and it cracked and we made it back to the shore. The law said Harry's death was an accident.'

'So there you go,' Parker said.

'What we're talking about now is an intruder.'

'An *alleged* intruder,' Parker said.

'Okay, so his body didn't fall through the sky-light on to my easel!'

'What took you so long, Mrs Logan?'

'To report it? I'll tell you Parker . . . Did anyone ever call you nosey?'

'A few times. Just like White is Chalky and tall folk are Lofty. I'll ask you again – what took you so long?'

'Male attitudes. Ask any woman living alone. She is treated with scepticism, Officer Parker. She is regarded by men as fair game, by women as a threat. *Did you hear Sarah Logan has seen* – boy, listen to that *seen* – *a rapist? What does she expect, painting pornographic pictures in that den of hers?*'

'So why did you finally call me?'

'Because the dog kept howling,' Sarah said inadequately.

'Mmmmm.'

'Because a Peeping Tom can get other ideas and there are other vulnerable women in town!'

'Okay, let's take a look at your studio.' He crushed the empty beer can in one hand.

'You didn't want to see it last time.'

'Last time was different,' he said.

Meaning that I wasn't unequivocally alone. She led the way past the butterfly house.

'Pretty,' Parker said, pausing as *Attacus atlas*, as big as a hand, fluttered past the inside of the glass wall. 'Can you tell male from female?'

'They can. Sight and scent. The male gives out the scent.'

'The opposite to humans.'

'Not always,' Sarah said, opening the door of the studio and standing back to observe Parker's reaction to the onslaught of female flesh in acrylic.

He nibbled at his thumb-nail. His teeth clicked together and he touched his fly as though he were adjusting his dress before leaving a washroom.

Wrenching his mind away from the paintings, he pointed to the sky-light. 'So that's where the alleged voyeur was.' He nodded to himself. 'Who do you think he was spying on, Mrs Logan? The nudes? The model? You?'

'Maybe he was checking the plumbing.'

'Why so hostile? You called me, remember?'

In truth she didn't know. Unless . . . *You will encounter strong opposition.* Was she creating it? She certainly wasn't relying too heavily on charm.

She said: 'You're right. I'm sorry.'

'Mind if I take a look on the roof?'

'Be my guest.'

She waited, listening to the scrape of his black brogues on the mildewed tiles. His face appeared at the sky-light and she hugged her arms round her breasts as though she were naked.

'Nothing,' he mouthed. And when he returned to the studio: 'No scratch marks, no broken tiles.'

'Maybe he wore sneakers?'

'All I could see from there were a couple of nudes – the one on the easel, mostly. Janice Gotthardt, isn't it?'

'As ever was.'

'And her husband doesn't care? I sure would,' before she had time to answer.

'But you're not married, are you, Officer Parker?'

'Not yet,' he winked. *Playing the field*, the wink said.

'Tell me, does Vic Gotthardt have a beer belly?'

'Matter of fact, he does. Why?'

'Intuition,' Sarah said, moving to the door.

'We're kind of buddies. As much as a cop can ever have friends outside the force. But I can't respect a guy who betrays his body like that.' Parker felt instinctively for a bicep beneath his tweed jacket. 'I don't pump iron or anything, but I take care of myself. I figure we owe it to ourselves. You exercise, Mrs Logan? You look pretty good.'

'I mix paints,' Sarah said.

'Matter of fact, I did some modelling once.'

Oh, shit, she thought.

'Clothed, you understand. But I don't see why a guy shouldn't pose in the nude. Not if he's looked after himself, got some muscles in the right places.' He nibbled at his thumb-nail again. Click. 'What do you think?'

'I'm fresh out of fig leaves,' she said, holding open the door.

Outside the butterfly house he paused once more. 'There's the big fella again. *Attacus atlas* – wasn't that what you called him?'

'Only lives for a week.'

'Sad son of a bitch. What does he do with his time?'

Fornicates, Sarah remembered. But she didn't let on.

First Vic Gotthardt. Then Sam Parker.

Sarah lay deep in a hot bath and flicked at the foam with thumb and middle finger.

Two ordinary macho guys who had never threatened her in any way. So why had she shown both of them sharp teeth?

She sank deeper into the water and watched the rainbow colours spinning on the bubbles.

It worried her.

Chapter Four

You will travel and meet old associates. The day will be relatively uneventful for a woman of your temperament, but as darkness falls . . .

Rebecca Cotton, of Polish extraction, tall with thrusting legs and fine, fair hair, also known as Athena, hesitated.
 Sometimes the power she exercised scared her.
 A senator didn't arrive for a crucial vote because Athena had warned him that flying might be hazardous.
 A Hollywood director trashed another *Casablanca* because on that day *all decisions are fallible.*
 A financial adviser told his clients to buy, buy, stock in a trucking company . . . *Today your perception will be acute.* And investors lost their shirts. 'Acute' doesn't mean positive, does it?
 A mayor, reading that *all indications for romance are favourable*, called on his mistress at an apartment that had been bugged that morning by the FBI.
 The president . . .
 But not just newsmakers. She worried about clients who were only known to their small circle of acquaintances. She had favourites, too, just like beloved characters in fiction: Piglet, or Mrs Gamp, or Jane Eyre.
 Sarah Logan for one.
 She left her computer and stared out of the window of her Manhattan penthouse. Far below she could see pedestrians following the strings of their destinies in the cold sunlight.
 Saw them from a star.

What they needed was guidance. But what if they were unduly influenced by the stars? That girl wearing a mustard yellow coat. *A day to follow your impulses.* Sees a friend across the street, darts in front of a cab which hits her . . . If she hadn't read her horoscope she would still be striding along the sidewalk.

Which, thank God, she still is.

How many of them butting into the future down there had already read their predictions in newspapers and magazines, heard them on TV or dial-the-stars phone numbers? Even cynics surreptitiously glanced at their forecasts, knew during cocktail hour whether they were intense Scorpios or reliable Taureans.

Still worrying, Rebecca Cotton lay on a couch beside the computer that was poised to print out Sarah Logan's prediction and stared at the stars painted on the dark blue ceiling.

She was fond of Sarah Logan because she had been her first client.

Had explained to her at their consultation – she didn't encourage further meetings – that if you could have photographed the heavens at the moment of your birth then that would be your horoscope. That it was the business of the astrologer to interpret all that *photographed* information and the subsequent movement of those planets in relation to the twelve fixed signs of the Zodiac.

She had explained, too, how the moon influences us. Reflecting the sun, the fount of energy, it controlled the tides, the flow of sap, including blood, our moods. Which was why astrologers took so much note of its movement around the earth: twenty-eight and a half days for one rotation and therefore two or so in each segment of the Zodiac. And when the moon was in Gemini the subject, Sarah, would be compelled towards spontaneous action. Creativity. Painting . . .

Rebecca had fluttered her fingers over the keyboard of the computer and read some of Sarah's analysis based on her chart.

You feel the flow of life and try to absorb other people's sentiments so that you can identify with the whole human experience.

There will be contradictions in your character but you must remember that Gemini is the Heavenly Twins, two personalities competing within the same body.

Your deep sympathy with Mankind sometimes overrules your instincts, especially when danger threatens.

After these prognostications Rebecca had inserted some generalizations about Geminians. Their charm, quick wit, adaptability, creativity. On the negative side: a tendency to take on too many interests at once, a low threshold of boredom . . .

Rebecca fed in the factors determining Sarah Logan's monthly horoscope. *Aggressive influences are directed against you, particularly from one person.*

You will be difficult in your attitude to those you believe are trying to intimidate you. Some people may wish you harm, so take great care!

Rebecca frowned at the painted stars.

Then she replaced the monthly horoscope with Sarah's prediction for today, Monday. When it was completed she printed it out and fed it into the fax.

A knock on the door: her assistant who believed, wrongly, that a timorous rap was less irritating than a robust blow.

The door opened before she had responded and a man pushed past her assistant, shut the door and locked it.

'Please,' he said, jerking his head towards the door, 'tell her not to call the police.'

'I think I'll tell her to *call* the police.'

'Your son is Libra, isn't he?'

Her finger rested on the button of the intercom. 'So?'

'*Tread warily if you want to avoid a minor mishap.* Maybe not so minor, Mrs Cotton?'

She pressed the button and told Carmen Barea from Puerto Rico to relax.

'Where did you get that prediction from?'

'You aren't the only star gazer in New York city, Mrs Cotton.' Beneath the jean jacket, soiled on one side as though he carried logs, he wore a black, roll-neck sweater. His poet's face was contradicted by cold wet eyes.

'Don't try and remember my face,' he said. 'I'm only the messenger.' His voice was phlegmy.

'What do you want?' And then: 'Where's my son?' trembling with delayed shock.

'He's just fine. At school by now. Geography first lesson, right? Only subject I ever made out with. How about you, Mrs Cotton?'

'How do I know he's all right?'

'Call the school.' He lit a black-tobacco cigarette and coughed smoke.

She dialled the school, knuckles polished white on the receiver. From a photograph on her desk Robbie smiled at her, basketball in his hands; *her* short-sighted blue eyes behind glasses, *her* soft fair hair skipping in the breeze.

Mrs Skipton was surprised that she had called, especially at this hour, her busiest. She told Rebecca to hold. The man in the black roll-neck coughed more smoke. Mrs Skipton's breathing on the phone . . . Robbie was just fine, sitting third row back in the first class of the morning, geography.

Rebecca replaced the receiver. Smiled back at Robbie at Point Judith at the mouth of Narragansett Bay on Rhode Island. The last vacation the three of them had spent together before the split.

'There you go,' the man in the roll-neck said.

'You said you were only the messenger. What's the message?'

Drawing his chair closer to the desk, words wrapped in smoke, he said: 'All in good time, Mrs Cotton. All in good time.'

Chapter Five

. . . as darkness falls be prepared for a glimpse into the dark side of life.

Which gave her the daylight hours anyway.

Sarah smartened herself up for the Big Apple – ranch mink and a rust-coloured Issey Miyake suit – and drove south in her modest black BMW. What she had to do was steer her thoughts away from the prediction, otherwise she would adapt to it. Hanging on for darkness, ferreting around in it for a glimpse . . .

So why don't you stop at the next call box, telephone Rebecca Cotton – Athena – and cancel the service? Sarah shook her head vehemently, startling the bald-headed driver of an oncoming station wagon into a swerve. The predictions will still exist *but I won't know what they are.*

She felt the icy lap of panic. A ballooning inside her skull. She gripped the wheel and searched for distraction.

The couple in the Pontiac ahead. Girl's head resting on the shoulder of the driver – the way she had sometimes rested her head on Harry's shoulder when she was tired.

What was it that affected her most about being alone again? a couple of women had asked. There you had it – *again*. The return to solitude that you believed you had discarded. A solitude of a different calibre because you had dropped your guard.

The emptiness of the bedroom. The weight of silence that pressed memories into one-dimensional prints. Discovery of possessions that, since his death, had lingered inanimately –

gold St Christopher medallion, Dracula teeth that he had worn at a dumb Halloween party, box of abandoned tubes of solidified paint, polka-dot tie, pipe with a charred bowl . . .

This new solitude, this sociological reversal, was always muted. Echoes swallowed by stillness, nips of perception instantly healed, sightings of shared joy eclipsed. Perhaps that was the essence of bereavement: the inability to recreate.

The solitariness also affected those couples who had regarded you as a unit. At first the spirit of requiem was more or less sincere, but gradually their attitudes changed. The men appraised you appreciatively, their women speculatively. Plainly there was something indecent about premature widowhood. Especially if the widow painted nudes.

Sarah overtook the Pontiac. The girl's eyes were closed but Sarah didn't believe she was asleep. The man who wore a bandit's moustache was smiling and Sarah guessed she was stroking him. She hoped the planets would be kind to them.

Across the river from the Pallisades Interstate Yonkers and the Bronx reared. She drove across George Washington Bridge and steered the BMW towards SoHo.

The gallery was in a sturdy block on West Broadway where, alongside Greene, Prince, Spring and Wooster Streets, art had set up its easel among relics of industry. In the window was an Alice Neel nude, but nothing so ambitious lay in the resonant chambers behind. In fact the disparate figure paintings had acquired the despondency of inattention.

She found Mike Kaplan crouched at his desk behind orderly piles of *Art Forum, Art in America* and *ARTnews*. He was planning her exhibition on sheets of cartridge paper.

'Hi.' He waved her to a chair. Aesthetic, astute, trim of moustache and body he would have looked good in police blues but favoured a lighter shade of denim.

'So how's it going?' she inquired.

'Just great.' Voice like chocolate buttons spilling. 'Mid-January, right? Big media coverage, lots of definite maybes.' He ran his fingers through his thick blue-black hair. '*New York Times, Newsday, Village Voice, Time, Newsweek, New Yorker, New York mag* . . . TV, radio, you got it. But what we need is a gimmick for the Philistines.'

'Maybe I should dress the nudes and appear stripped?'
'If only Harry –'
'I know,' she said. 'He would have thought of something.' She compressed her lips to quell the trembling in the lower one.
'You still –'
'Probably always will.'
'I never appreciated just how much he contributed. Flair . . . I've got the dull grey stuff but he could light this place up.'
'I know,' Sarah said. 'He lights up a winter day.'
'Lit. He's dead, Sarah. You can't –'
'Live in the past, I know it. But why did he die?'
'We know *how* he died,' Kaplan said, wiping at the geometric boundaries of his moustache with the tips of his fingers. 'He drowned.'
'But what was he doing in the lake?'
'We've been through this –'
'A thousand times. I know that too.'
'Glass of wine?' He produced a bottle of Chablis, coldly sweating, from an ice-bucket inside his desk.
'I don't think so. You go ahead.'
Kaplan, pouring himself half a glass of wine and added soda. 'He drove into Manhattan, no question. And he intended to drive back . . .'
'But he didn't, did he?'
Then maybe a little decadence, Harris permitting.
'Because,' Kaplan said, finding wine and soda on his moustache with the tip of his tongue, 'his car wouldn't start. So he took the Hudson River Valley railroad from Grand Central to Poughkeepsie where he took a cab . . .'
'The driver never came forward.'
'Scared? Moonlighting?'
'Who dropped him beside the lake maybe half a mile from our house.'
'Where he used to think. When he was worried. He was worried, you testified to that.'
'So what was he doing in the water?'
'You know the theory as well as I do. A kid, a teenager, had fallen through the ice and Harry tried to rescue him. The kid made it back to shore, Harry didn't. There was evidence of

surface fractures on the ice both sides of the lake before it froze really deep.'

'And the teenager didn't come forward either.'

'Scared shitless,' Kaplan said, taking a sip of wine.

'They should have dragged the lake, then.'

'Why, for God's sake? A man drives into New York city and disappears. Leaves his automobile in a garage. Why should the cops drag a lake half a mile from his house?'

'Sometimes I hear voices near the lake,' Sarah said.

'I know,' Kaplan said gently, 'from the Indian burial ground. The fact remains he drowned and the law said it was an accident.'

'And, sure, the insurance company paid out, God bless them. I would rather have lived on grits . . .'

'Hush,' Kaplan said. 'Now you just hush.'

'So what's your horoscope for today? *You will meet a charming shrink who will turn into a frog?*' Deacon smeared Beluga caviar on to a bliny.

'No need to jump like one when you see the check,' Sarah said. 'My treat, remember?'

A waiter poured Georgian white and mineral water. The Russian Tea Room was packed as though, vicariously, everyone wanted to share the vicissitudes of the late Soviet Union. It was certainly better than lining up for sprouting potatoes in the central market in Moscow.

Deacon rubbed his hands together, the way he did before a consultation. She still wondered what, under hypnosis, he had netted from her self-conscious. Childhood tantrums, teenage rebellion . . . all the platitudes . . .

Had she told him the absolute mundane truth, that she had wanted to be friends with her parents? To walk with them in fields of poppies, to share storms, to walk out of bad movies together? They hadn't sent her away to school: they did worse, separated her from their lives inside the household, her behavioural attitudes discussed with other visiting parents.

If only, just once, they had whooped back when she had whooped! But lawyers do not whoop. Nor do their wives. Not even on the golf course. Sarah hoped sincerely that, under psychoanalysis, she had not revealed anything as prosaic as that.

The waiter served sturgeon casseroled with tomatoes and vegetables for her, chicken kiev for Deacon, and departed across the red-walled dining-room that shone with polished brass, humming sadly to himself.

'Wants to go back to St Petersburg,' Deacon said. 'Worried what brand of servitude is going to replace tsarism and communism. No Russian is happy until he's unhappy.' He forked a piece of chicken dripping with butter. 'You don't seem very happy, Sarah.'

'Would you, if you were about to be treated to a glimpse of the dark side of life?'

Deacon sighed and chewed, worry and hunger like cloud shadows followed by light on his wise, hawkish face. 'Today's predictions? Forget it. A woman is told not to go out in the rain – her car will skid, maybe – so she stays at home and the house is struck by lightning.'

'Nothing wrong with signposts.'

'Unless they lead you into a river.'

Or a lake, she thought.

'I've got some time this afternoon,' Deacon said, waving at a beautiful woman with frightened eyes set wide apart in a powder white face.

'A patient?'

'We shrinks have got to be careful,' Deacon said enigmatically. 'Will you come round?'

'Hopefully never again. As a patient, that is.' She touched one of his big hands that looked like clubs when he occasionally clenched them during delicate incisions into the psyche.

'Call me tomorrow,' Deacon said over tea poured from a samovar. 'Meanwhile don't go looking for that glimpse. I thought you were cured.'

'You filled the void,' she said, 'when Harry disappeared ... died. You were the friend. We walked in a poppy field together.' Sometimes she could be as inscrutable as a psychiatrist.

She paid the check and walked briskly out of the Russian Tea Room, trespassing in the contemplation of the woman with the frightened eyes who was staring through the diners, through the walls. To St Petersburg?

She drove slowly, the crawl that police look for when they're out drunk-hunting.

Timing the fall of darkness.

When precisely *was* that?

Sunlight faded, wisps of mist assembled at the foot of the wooded slopes of the Hudson. She took a left and Holyfield presented itself like a museum village, like Monroe with its apothecary and blacksmiths. She heard healthy shouting from the direction of the lacrosse field. Parker would doubtless be there controlling the sparse flow of traffic. Sarah guessed that, whenever the safety of schoolgirls was in question, Parker would be there lending a hand.

She passed the forest containing the bones of the Iroquois at rest after they had finished fighting for the English and playing lacrosse.

The pointed gable of the house broke the line of paper birch tree-tops. A fine, shingled, comfortable home. She drove the BMW into the garage, lingered behind the wheel smelling leather spiced with gasoline, waiting for darkness to fall, as though it descended like rain. Finally she opened the door of the car, let it close with a thick clunk and headed for the house, checking the studio and butterfly house on the way.

The door of the studio was closed. She listened to her feet crunching gravel, then her whispered footsteps on the grass.

Wings fluttered, as softly as eyelids closing, in the butterfly house.

She reached the kitchen door, heard the windshield wipe of Harris's tail and his nostril whine. The key fitted snugly and Harris was upon her.

Sitting beneath the herbs hanging from the ceiling, she waited for peace. Instead a flutter of unease like a swirl of dried petals inside her chest. She went to the window. Beyond the square of light on the lawn another faint glow: she hadn't switched off the light in the garage.

Leave it!

No, that would be confounding her resolution and the glimpse of whatever it was would remain there. Nevertheless she took Harris, snuffling, with her.

Halfway to the garage he sensed a presence among the birch trees and bounded away in pursuit, barking intrepidly.

When the barking stopped she heard him excavating in the fallen leaves.

She switched off the light to the garage. On the way back she pushed the door of the studio with the tip of her index finger. It opened.

But she had locked it, hadn't she? *So what you do now, Sarah, is run like hell to the house and call the police.*

She curved her wrist round the door, found the old-fashioned switch. Stopped breathing. Heard the powerful beat of her heart. Pressed the switch down.

Janice Gotthardt's nipples had been cut from the canvas and light shone through the holes. Her crotch had been slashed many times with a knife and the knife itself protruded from the shadow of the natural cleft. Daubed in red across the top of the unfinished painting: YOU NEXT.

Sarah switched off the light and made her way back to the house; observed, she felt, by the false eyes on the wings of *Attacus atlas* that were designed to frighten predators. Harris bounded up and placed his wet nose in the cup of her hand. A star fell. A death.

Chapter Six

A challenge. Watch for duplicity on the part of advisers ...

Tuesday.
 Parker arrived at lunchtime, apologizing for the delay but reminding Sarah that perverts were not high on his list of priorities.
 What was? Communal safety, maintenance of law and order, showing the uniform? Which he wasn't now: the same tweed jacket.
 He pulled the knife from Janice's crotch, taking elaborate care not to touch the bone handle. 'Recognize it?' He dangled it by the blade.
 'A kitchen knife. Could be mine – anybody's.'
 'Let's check, huh?'
 She rumaged in the second drawer down beside the sink. The carver was missing; same bone handle as the knife Parker held by the blade.
 'Mind if we print you, Mrs Logan?' Parker laid the knife on a dish cloth. 'We have to check every angle. Looks real bad if someone refuses. And it *is* your knife.'
 Sarah shrugged okay.
 'You went to the kitchen last night before returning to the garage?'
 'I told you, I noticed the garage light was still burning.'
 'Let's take another look at the studio,' Parker said.
 YOU NEXT. 'Who hates you?' he asked.
 'You never know, do you, Officer Parker? People smile at you, shake hands, kiss your cheek even. And then, when your back's turned –'

'They put the knife in. I know it. You'd be surprised how much resentment there is, even in a small town like Holyfield. In my business I see it every day.' He placed one finger at the confluence of the slashes on Janice Gotthardt's body, nibbled at the thumbnail of his free hand with teeth that looked older than the rest of him.

'Doing your kind of painting, you must come across a lot of resentment,' he said, withdrawing his finger from the painting and, thank God, not placing it anywhere else.

'I sense it, sure.'

'You know, Holyfield is a clean town.'

'Painting nudes is dirty?'

'Not the way I see it. But the women . . . Maybe they figure the female body should be treated with more respect.'

'We only dress, Officer Parker, to keep warm.'

'In summer?'

'To keep cool. Have they asked you, these women, to warn me off?'

'I hear things, is all. First the peeper, now this,' pointing at the mutilated painting.

'They know about this already?'

'No secret, is it?'

'So what do they want me to paint – trees?'

'Male nudes would be okay, I guess. In any case they needn't know.' He made his offer candidly, arms folded, fingers clasping his biceps.

'Supposing someone did that to you,' she nodded at the painting.

'Wouldn't need no knife.' He smiled with burgeoning candour. 'Not sticking out there anyway,' pointing.

'Better get that kitchen knife to the lab, Officer Parker. You can take my prints later.'

Asshole, she thought as he walked to his car cradling the knife delicately in the dishcloth. You wouldn't have talked like that to a married woman. But a widow was fair game.

Her next visitors were Vic and Janice Gotthardt.

'Jesus H. Christ,' exclaimed Vic Gotthardt, staring at the painting, small voice emerging from the paunchy body that Sarah had envisaged. 'How sick can you get?'

Janice, wearing scuffed knee-length boots and off-white jeans, put her hands to her breasts. 'Oh my,' she said, swaying. 'Oh my.' Backing towards the door, she opened her mouth to the cold breeze that, coming from the east, brought with it the gluey smell of sap and sawdust from the mill. Her husband lingered inside studying Sarah's work, a connoisseur.

Emerging, he hoisted his belly. 'Look, I'm broad-minded, okay? But that . . . sick, sick, *sick*! I can't let Janice go on posing, now can I?' He placed one proprietal hand on the back of his wife's neck and Sarah noticed that one of her eyes was swollen, as though it had received a flat-handed swipe from the same hand.

'Just a few more sessions, Mr Gotthardt. You see, I've got to start the painting again. *Got* to finish it. I mustn't be defeated. Do you understand that?'

'"You next" *Who* next?'

'Me, I guess.'

'Aren't you running scared?'

'Most women have hassles from a weirdo at some time in their lives.'

Janice said: 'I'm scared, I don't mind telling you.' The swollen eye contained a glimmer of conspiracy. *You don't fool me, Sarah Logan.*

Her husband removed his hand from her neck. 'Tell you something, Sarah, it's really weird knowing your wife strips off in front of another woman.'

'Gets to you, does it, Mr Gotthardt?'

Janice's hand went to her cheek and her fingers crawled to her puffed eye.

'Times are hard,' her husband said. 'We need the dough.'

'Then you wouldn't mind –'

'You're paying ten bucks an hour, right? Make it twenty. For art's sake.'

Sarah turned to Janice. 'What do you say?'

'I say, "Who's this Art!"' Janice said and her slitted eye smiled.

At 3.30 Sarah reported to Parker, now showing the uniform once more, to have her fingerprints taken. Then she adjourned to the library to join the solitary men in its snug time warp. Mary Breeden, chairwoman of Holyfield Women's Guild, president of Holyfield History Society, reigned here, vetting the content of the novels on loan, guarding the inner sanctum where three mauve and white-beaded Iroquois wampum belts and ceremonial masks were stored out of sight.

Sarah jointed two habitués wearing windbreakers and lumberjack shirts who were staring glassy-eyed at books about the Six Nations Iroquois Confederacy that had once sprawled from the Atlantic to Mississippi, from the Carolinas to the Gulf of St. Lawrence in Canada, discarding small artefacts like Holyfield as history squeezed it. Sarah sat beside them at an oak table opposite a copy of a mid-eighteenth-century painting of Iroquois warriors playing a brawling game of lacrosse. She admired the play of muscles stroked by the artist, Charles Deas, and the infinite sky – vast lakes of it inside sunset clouds – and she made some notes.

As she wrote, one of her companions laid his grey head on a map in his book and breathed gently across Lake Huron. Mary Breeden, a handsome woman with tightly combed flaxen hair who bore the frailties of others with fortitude, shook him by the shoulder. 'Come on, Tom. You, too, Harvey – this isn't a dormitory.'

Obediently, they shut their books, replaced them and, wearing fragile smiles, made their way into the alien outdoors.

'I let them stay as long as I can,' she explained to Sarah. 'But when they fall asleep . . . well, it looks untidy, doesn't it?' She glanced at the painting of the Iroquois. 'Fine-looking men, weren't they?'

Like most citizens of Holyfield Sarah knew the history of the confederacy as thoroughly as the history of the United States. How most Iroquois had supported the British against the French, then against the Americans in the War of Independence. How George Washington had ordered General John Sullivan to attack their heartland in the north. How they scattered – to Quebec and Ontario, to Wisconsin, New York State, Oklahoma . . .

She knew that the confederacy still existed, its capital at Onondaga near Syracuse in upstate New York where passports for the Iroquois, or Haudenosaunee, as they called themselves, were issued, where the symbolic Fire That Never Dies still burned. She also knew that they had recently beaten the bejeysus out of the English at lacrosse.

'Couldn't take their liquor,' Mary Breeden said. 'But they could teach us a thing or two about morals.'

'Beautiful bodies,' Sarah said.

'I'm sure you're right.' She laid one hand on Sarah's shoulder.

Sarah frowned. 'Can't you see that for yourself?'

'Finely muscled, that's for sure. Not posing . . .' And Sarah thought: *Here it comes.*

'You're a fine painter, Sarah.'

'Thank you,' said Sarah who wasn't so sure, suspected sometimes that she painted merely to instil life and colour into a void, and plagiarised Alice Neel – if that were possible. Hadn't *her* sailor husband slashed sixty of her paintings. Cold lapped the shores of her mind again.

'Are you all right, dear?'

Sarah said she was okay.

'A fine painter. But, dare I say it, misguided.'

'Nudes?'

'We want you to become famous, Sarah. We want Holyfield to bask in that fame. But notoriety – now we don't want that, do we?'

'You mean the Peeping Tom? The mutilation?'

'Ugly,' Mary Breeden said. She shivered and sat at the table, poised to forgive. 'Unnecessary.'

'I can't be responsible for the behaviour of perverts.'

'Aren't you perhaps encouraging them?'

'You mean Rubens encouraged deviates?'

'I think that remark is a little facetious.'

Sarah noticed that Mary Breeden had brown eyes. With her colouring they should have been blue.

'Are you ashamed of your body, Mrs Breeden?' For her age, fifty or so, she was trim enough.

'We are as God made us. None of us has any cause for shame. Which doesn't mean to say that we should –'

'Flaunt ourselves?'

'If you wish.'

'All my models come to me voluntarily. You'd be surprised how many volunteer. Have you ever considered modelling, Mrs Breeden?'

Mary Breeden stood up. No theatrical outrage; Sarah almost admired her for it. 'I realize you're upset by what has occurred. We'll talk again when you're more . . . composed. For the time being I'll leave you with your game of lacrosse. The original French settlers called it that because the stick looks like a bishop's staff.'

Smiling courageously, she returned to her desk.

In the street, opposite the offices of the *Holyfield Banner* and Griswold's drug store, Sarah met Sam Parker.

'Thought I'd let you know, Mrs Logan, that I've done some preliminary work on those prints. Nothing definite, you understand, that's Albany's baby. But I dusted the handle of the knife and took a Polaroid of the prints, and I took a Polaroid of your prints – and guess what? They look as though they might match.'

In the comfortable, shingled house Sarah Logan watches a silent black and white movie, *The Lady Vanishes*. Watching is the right word – she hasn't turned on the volume on the remote control.

She leaves Michael Redgrave and Margaret Lockwood soundlessly mouthing and, pushing aside the drapes of quiet, glides to the kitchen where Harris is asleep in his basket. She picks up the red telephone attached to the wall and calls Mike Kaplan. Mike is heavily engaged with, he says, a writer from *ARTnews*. Can he call her back . . . a pause . . . say 9.30 tomorrow morning?

She calls Ben Deacon. An answering machine and she doesn't even wait for the beep.

Calls her parents in Ford Lauderdale. Her mother. 'Darling, we're just in the middle of a rubber of bridge . . .'

Hangs up.

Retires to bed taking a sleeping capsule to condense the hours before the gentle whirr of the fax in the morning.

Chapter Seven

The sun is in your solar seventh house and it is an important time for close relationships. A propitious day for repairing the ravages of the past . . .

Bland. But Rebecca Cotton wasn't displeased with the prediction for Sarah Logan because in a way she shared it. Same date of birth, 1st June, 1962: therefore both Gemini, the Heavenly Twins, sharing the same element, water; same quality, mutability; same planet, Mercury; same metal, mercury; same stone, tiger's eye; same opposite, Sagittarius, the Archer. Both born in New Jersey. Only the actual time of birth and the longitude and lattitude differed; but the difference was marginal.

Another day without any word from the man with the poet's face. How long was it now? She consulted the wall calendar hedged with the signs of the Zodiac. Maybe he had merely been a mindless crank?

She placed the prediction on her desk ready to fax: one of fifty which, with the help of Carmen Barea, she transmitted every day on her three machines. Five hundred dollars a week per client; one million two hundred thousand a year. Not so terrific when you considered the rent of the penthouse, Robbie's school fees . . .

She worked on the horoscope of a member of the House of Representatives, one of those who had been involved in the dud cheque scandal. His name was now linked with a real estate scam and the prediction hinted that he should resign. So there was one prophecy that wouldn't come true!

But more often than not they did. Consider Jacqueline Stallone, Sylvester's mother, who had predicted a grave accident for the husband of Princess Caroline of Monaco – he had *died* in an accident! – and had forecast that Britain's Queen Elizabeth would not abdicate. Then the Queen herself virtually confirmed the forecast.

Carmen Barea knocked timidly on the door and came in with the material she had taken home with her to study in her cramped home in East Harlem: blank birth charts, ephemera containing the position of the sun, moon and planets at midday GMT every day, tables of the houses, birth dates of clients, variations for those born in a cusp – the fringes of a birth sign.

'I made out the chart and horoscope for Sarah Logan,' she said, Spanish accent emerging prettily from her lips. 'Just like you said – to compare with the one you've done.'

'Okay, I'll look at it when we've sent today's batch.'

'Coffee, Mrs Cotton?'

'Coffee would be great,' Rebecca said, as she said every morning at 6 a.m. She watched Carmen leave the room, hair shining blue-black, looking like an extra from a revival of *West Side Story*, but a serious student of astrology nonetheless, isolating herself from the brawl of her family when she studied at home.

Rebecca worked steadily and at 6.30 she and Carmen Barea began to transmit the predictions.

Repairing the ravages of the past . . .

At 1 p.m. she and Robbie were meeting Will at F.A.O. Schwarz toy store for some pre-Christmas viewing – it was the first time the three of them had been out together since the split. Rebecca had been tempted to work out a forecast for Will, a Taurus, but that would have been a betrayal, because it was her success as an astrologer that had divided them. *The steady Taurus male does not appreciate a woman taking the initiative.* Certainly not a professor of law at Columbia. *The Taurus man enjoys a homely home.* An East Side penthouse in midtown Manhattan? The Taurus professor of law prefers a plump divorcee with a house that probably smells of cats on Long Island! A Libra who *always puts her man top of her priorities*.

At moments like this Rebecca Cotton wishes she had never taken up with the stars. Wishes she had become a painter. Like Sarah Logan.

Then she thinks, hell, no: decision remains the right of the individual, one of the tenets of astrology.

Before the split they used to drive to the Catskills for the first snow of winter. She goes to the window and rain weeps against the glass.

She picks up the chart Carmen Barea has made out for Sarah Logan. And her forecast for the day. *A good time to right a wrong . . .*

Rebecca compares it with her prediction. Carmen Barea is inexperienced but she is coming along just fine. She could become a good astrologer if she believes. It is the *if* that bothers Rebecca.

Software for his Apple computer. Rebecca and Will itemized it on their lists and glanced at each other. Their son was going to be an electronics whizzkid.

Robbie, fair-haired and delicately boned, foraged ahead of them. A remote controlled model of a Ferrari. Or a Formula One racing driver? Console video game. Another Einstein?

Outside the store, its pre-Christmas windows thronged with toys, they caught a cab to Peng's on East 44th because, after hamburgers, Chinese food was what Robbie liked best. They talked briefly while he was in the washroom.

'So how's the witch?' Rebecca said.

'Sprucing up her broom.'

'To give the house *another* purge?'

'Nothing wrong with a clean, comfortable home.'

If they were strangers, how would she have classified Will? Broker, banker, lawyer . . . His spectacles glinted wisely enough, and his brown eyes constantly assessed from his lean face, and his charcoal suit was sober but, no, he wasn't an attorney: not calculating enough, notes of irreverence in his voice. And yet . . . Only an exceptionally astute observer would have partnered jurisprudence with flippancy and made a professor of law out of him.

And what would Will have made of me? Ex-model without her wigcase – perceptive – who had progressed to . . . what?

Madison Avenue executive in her lime green Giorgio Armani outfit? Astrologer never!

'My home isn't exactly dirty,' she heard herself saying.

'Except that it isn't a home. I was thinking about buying Robbie a basketball net – but in a penthouse?'

'What about the cute little house on Long Island?'

'We've already got one,' Will said.

We!

'You know I never objected to astrology,' he said.

'To what, then?'

'You know what.'

'Me making the bucks?'

'I do all right.'

'I know you do.' She touched his hand. 'I'm sorry.'

'I certainly don't disbelieve in the stars. Only an idiot would. But that doesn't mean I believe.'

'You don't know whether you're for the defence or prosecution. No wonder you took to teaching law.'

'That's the trouble with courtroom law. How can both sides be right? Well they can. That's why I quit. It is the law that decides one has to be right, one wrong, and that's why the law is an ass.'

'You mean *we* are right and wrong.'

'My case rests,' Will said, polishing his spectacles with a silk handkerchief.

'Robbie's taking a long time.'

'He wants us to talk. Without shouting, like we should have done long ago.'

'Do you shout, you and the witch?'

'No,' Will said. 'That's *our* trouble.'

'Trouble?'

'It's tough at Christmas, isn't it? Christmas Day, you have Robbie in the morning, I have him in the afternoon. Or vice versa?'

'Couldn't we have him . . . together?'

'Tricky,' Will said.

'I understand.'

'You don't.'

'I do, really.'

'Boy, we really fuck up, don't we, us adults?'

'Okay, let's order,' Robbie said. 'Did you know Mr Peng was once the best cook in Taiwan?' He sat down and Rebecca thought that for someone who had spent so long in the washroom his hands didn't look that clean.

After the meal they took in a movie: Kevin Costner's *Robin Hood* which had re-emerged from the greenwood for the run-up to Christmas. Then the worst time of all, the weekend parting.

'Okay,' Will said in the rain-swept street, 'I'll take him to school Monday morning.'

'Maybe next weekend,' Rebecca said, 'if it snows . . .'

'Maybe.'

The three of them huddled together beneath his umbrella as black as a judge's gown.

She kissed Robbie. 'Be good.'

Robbie said he always was. He climbed into the cab, followed by Will.

'Don't let him trip over the broomstick,' Rebecca whispered to Will. She waved as the cab took off, leaving her alone on the busy sidewalk.

She put up her own umbrella and began to walk in the general direction of the penthouse. 'That's our trouble,' he had said. What sort of trouble?

It was dusk when she reached her block, powdered rain gusting down the street from the East River, to be greeted by the man with the poet's face.

'How was Robin? Still robbing the rich to give to the poor? Good old Robin. We could do with a few like him in the Bronx. The kid enjoy it?'

'What do you want?' She had lowered the umbrella and the rain was cold on her face.

'Just keeping in touch.' He wasn't smoking but she could smell tobacco on his breath. 'And I have a message for you – *not long now*. That's the message. Nice kid, Robbie,' he said, 'wouldn't want any harm to come to him.' Showing her the knife in his gloved hand.

In her studio Sarah Logan, who had decided that she didn't want Janice Gotthardt to sit for her anymore – no more consultations with Vic Gotthardt – began to repair *the ravages of the past* on the mutilated canvas.

She pulled the rents at the crotch together and glued them from the back. The nipples were trickier; she cut jigsaw pieces of canvas to fit the apertures, stuck adhesive strips on the rear surface, pressed the two pieces into place so that they stuck to the strips.

When the glue was dry she began to paint: gaps for the nipples, rents at the crotch. She decided to call the painting *Nude Slashed*.

Chapter Eight

The light of childhood in her bedroom. First snow, the faintest and freshest of blue shining through the window, cleansing the night and all it had contained. Snowflakes hesitating.

Sarah languished beneath the covers for a few moments, shedding dreams, burrowing into youth: the gasp of cold outside the kitchen door, the quilted silence and the touch of a snowflake on your eyelash.

Then she remembered it was Sunday.

Now the emptiest of days. No smell of coffee as he padded around the kitchen in his moulting robe, no sections of the *NY Times* scattered across the bed, no rustling sex beneath the sections, no apologies to God for missing church, no brunch . . .

Snowflakes peered into the bedroom. She levered herself out of bed, put on the sensible robe and went into the kitchen where Harris reminded her that he at least was still there.

She opened the door and he leaped into the garden, trying to take the snow by surprise. Ahead was the butterfly house, sweaty dark and insular in the assembling white.

She glanced at the wall clock, minute hand stuttering. Her horoscope, later on Sundays, was due in seven minutes. She made coffee. Harris returned, shedding snow.

She fried two eggs and toasted bread while listening to a newscast on the radio – former Soviet republics at each other's throats, a gunman who had run amok in San Diego, the weather . . .

Returning to the bedroom, she put on old clothes and boots and tramped round the garden, thinking how soiled the trunks of the silver birches were against the snow, like old slippers in a shoe shop. When she got back to the house the horoscope was two minutes overdue, fax machine in her study beside the red telephone inanimate.

She poured more coffee, listening to the fluttering beat of the wall clock. Deciding to light a fire, she watched moths of flame creep along the kindling wood to the logs: picked up a silver-framed photograph of Harry wearing his Crombie, granny scarf, spectacles and the hat with the dashing brim.

Twenty minutes.

Well, it happened. Astrologers could be late like everyone else . . . Especially on Sunday.

The snow was making cushions in the corners of the window panes. She washed and dried a few dishes, changed the sheets on the bed.

Half an hour.

Magnanimously, Sarah decided to allow Athena another thirty minutes. She stripped off her clothes and took a shower, refusing as always to dwell on the shower scene in *Psycho*. Then she examined her face in the mirror: grey eyes set wide apart so that she looked startled when she was merely pleasantly surprised; an incipient line from the nose to the left corner of her mouth which she tried to erase with one finger; high cheekbones – they would bunch like apples when she was old; chestnut hair that, combed wet, imparted a false air of innocence. The face of an artist. Pity she wasn't a better one.

Wearing another robe – Chinese dragons – she padded downstairs. Nothing. Fax as obdurate as stone.

One hour, thirty-five minutes.

She typed a message. *Grateful if you would transmit my prediction now, as I have an important engagement in Albany.* She inserted the sheet of paper into the fax and punched out the number in New York. The machine bleeped. Engaged. Or unobtainable?

She left it to re-dial automatically and went on an inspection tour of the old house with its built-to-last furniture waxed with lavender-smelling polish and glimmers of brass in unexpected places. On the window-ledge outside the kitchen two pigeons pouted indignantly at the falling snow.

When she returned to the study the fax machine had used up its redials. She tried again then dressed for the second time – in jeans and shaggy jersey from Bloomingdales – and walked across the lawn to the studio to inspect *Nude Slashed*.

On her way back she checked the butterfly house. Wings encapsulated in the polarized tropics were as bright as jockey silks against the snow.

She entered the study with exaggerated nonchalance. The message sat there untransmitted.

Only one solution: use that antique relic of communications, the telephone. Even though Rebecca Cotton wouldn't like it, had in fact warned against personalizing the conclusions of the planets.

She extracted the unlisted number – 'Only to be used in emergencies' – from her computer and punched it out.

An answering service!

Her stomach lurched. But this, of course, was crazy, so she put on her beaver jacket, gave Harris a friendly whack on his flank, told the pigeons that communications were more reliable in their day, strode purposefully across the lawn to the garage and drove into Holyfield, arriving in time for the service in St Peter's Episcopalian Church.

In the front pews sat a prayer of women in decent clothes with matching husbands – women always seemed to dominate a congregation – Mary Breeden suffering the sinners around her with fortitude.

Sarah knelt as the minister led them in prayer for 'some of the fine, upright citizens of our community who are nevertheless misguided'. Mary Breeden looked round, tight flaxen fair hair undisturbed by the movement.

Outside the church she said: 'I'm so glad you were there for the sermon, Sarah.'

'Did you write it?'

Mary Breeden laughed; two other women laughed with her. 'Have the police found out who cut your painting?'

Cut. The first time the word had been used in the context of the Janice Gotthardt nude.

'Or the Peeping Tom, have they traced him?'

'Not yet, Mrs Breeden. But they will, they will.'

'I do hope so. Not the sort of person we want in Holyfield. Perhaps he came from, you know . . .' angling her eyes in the direction of the sawmill and its environs.

'If you'll excuse me . . .'

'If, of course, he existed at all.'

Sarah drove to the Silver Springs where she drank two Bloody Marys and lingered over a pot roast. What would the prediction have forecast if it had arrived? *Be wary of a confrontation with the enemy?*

When she left the restaurant the snow had almost stopped falling, a few flakes swirling like blind insects.

She approached the fax with a stylish display of indifference.

Nothing.

She activated the answering machine.

Mike Kaplan's chocolate voice: 'Hi, Sarah. Great news. Michael Kimmelman of the *Times* might be coming. But we still need a gimmick for the sensationals. Anyway, call me back, huh?'

The next message. Wispy voice. '*You next.*'

Nothing more.

She made her way to the studio. The fallen snow had thawed a little then re-frozen and it crunched beneath her boots. She locked the door and removed *Nude Slashed* from the easel, replacing it with a blank canvas. She mixed acrylics into a pale flesh tone and, glancing only once at the skylight, began to paint because there was nothing else she could do.

Chapter Nine

A void in your life will be filled. Be prepared to spend money because Mars is in your second house. An ambitious day which will culminate with unexpected freedom . . .

No doubt about the void being filled: the prediction itself had done just that. Relief spread like a warm stain.

Sarah dressed exuberantly. *Be prepared to spend money?* There were several outstanding bills and she could settle those. Insurance, tax, Mastercharge . . . and she had agreed to advance Mike Kaplan cash against sales from her exhibition because he certainly wasn't out of recession yet.

She unlocked the kitchen door for Harris and made lemon tea instead of coffee, fancying the tartness on her tongue. The pigeons were still on the ledge and snow was still on the ground with a thaw-and-freeze sheen to it.

An ambitious day? She would plan a schedule of innovative nudes, *Nude Slashed* at the helm.

Unexpected freedom? She shrugged it away: just let it happen. As for 'You next' on the answering machine – well, every woman living alone had to expect obscene calls and that wasn't so disgusting, was it?

She called the Gotthardts.

'A deal's a deal,' she told Vic Gotthardt, 'So I'm sending you a check for sixty dollars.'

'I'm sorry, I don't –'

'I decided not to do the painting again so I'm paying you for three sessions.'

A pause. A hoist of the belly? Then: 'We had an understanding, right? If it's anything to do with Janice's eye – well, that's healed now . . .'

'Janice was a good model, no mistake. But I can't go on painting the same woman all the time, now can I, Mr Gotthardt?'

'Why not? Women are all built the same, aren't they?'

Sarah grimaced at the phone. 'Okay, eighty dollars.'

'Trying to buy me off, Sarah?'

'For what, for God's sake?'

'Work it out for yourself, Sarah.'

'Mrs Logan.'

'Okay, Mrs Logan, figure it out.'

'Eighty dollars,' she said and hung up.

She made out a cheque for a hundred, put it in an ordinary envelope and addressed it to Janice Gotthardt – who would probably get another swipe on the eye, come what may. She wrote the other cheques, including one for five thousand dollars for Mike Kaplan and one for one thousand for the Society of Distressed Artists which was also the only beneficiary of her will – a considerable sum since the insurance company's pay-out on Harry's life policy. Then she went to Holyfield to mail them, adjourning afterwards to Noveck's soda fountain for a strawberry milkshake. Ambrose Moon was there and he beckoned her to his table.

'You look worried,' he said.

'Quite the opposite,' Sarah replied, sipping the lipstick-tasting milkshake.

'Are you sure?' Ambrose Moon, who looked not unlike Nelson Mandela, massaged the graceful, stick-like fingers of his left hand with the thumb and forefinger of his right. 'That's not what your body was telling me.'

'How's the book on gestures coming along, Mr Moon?'

'Just great.' He gestured with his right hand, opening the palm. 'People figure I should be staying in an Italian community. Right – up to a point. *Wow*,' a loose-wristed shake of his right hand, 'and *Get the hell out of it*,' pushing at air with the same hand. 'Obvious, you know. But here I get the gestures of repression. Evasions from lips, the truth in the hands and the feet and the angles of the head.'

'So why did you think I was worried?'

'The shoulders,' Ambrose Moon said, sipping his root beer. 'Lifted, tense.'

She let her shoulders droop. 'So what do you see in Holyfield?'

'I see people hiding, Mrs Logan.'

'Hiding from who? From *whom*?' Ambrose Moon made her nervous.

'From themselves. We all try it, you know. Here, they barricade themselves behind the Iroquois. Those lacrosse rackets – some gesture!'

'Can you tell when people are lying?'

'You look at the crossed leg, Mrs Logan. It swings.'

Sarah's hand went to her shin but it was motionless. 'Hypocrisy?'

'A curve of the finger. Waiting to see if you've been caught out.'

'A lot of curved fingers in Holyfield, huh, Mr Moon?'

'Hypocrisy's tricky. You see, most times people are kidding themselves. Like I said, hiding.'

'Snobbishness?'

'Chin lifted, eyes often partially closed. Reference Saitz and Cervenka in their *Handbook of Gestures*.'

'Was I lying when I said I wasn't worried?'

'No,' Ambrose Moon said. 'And that puzzled me because you *are* worried. Your shoulders said so. Know what I think?'

She shook her head.

'I think you are worried but something's happened to dispel the worry. Temporarily perhaps.'

'Or forever.'

'Watch your leg, Mrs Logan,' Ambrose Moon said. 'It's beginning to swing.'

Leaving behind the neuroses of Holyfield, Sarah drove west to the first mounds of the Catskills, vaguely aware of a green car behind her. Snow lay thinly between the pines and in the pale sunlight it looked warm – until, stopping, she opened the window and smelled the cold. With the cold came a mild attack of panic – why, she could not determine.

She drove on to Woodstock, stopping at Woodstock Artists' Association Gallery where they were staging an exhibition of Abbot Henderson Thayer's paintings from the Gilded Era: noble and virginal women portrayed by an artist so obsessed by purity that he wouldn't allow his children to go to school. The women were also fully clothed, in marked contrast to the work of Sarah Kathleen Logan. Sarah didn't think Thayer, who died in 1921, would have taken to Janice Gotthardt.

Why, being an avant-garde gallery, were they exhibiting such paintings? 'You've got to project contrasts,' an inscrutable young man with a downy beard said.

'Supposing I were to rip way that . . . that shroud she's wearing?'

'Come again?'

'It doesn't matter,' Sarah said.

She went to another gallery on Tinker Street, the Bell, to look at nudes painted by Beryl Kranz, the Brooklyn-born painter who had emigrated to Spain. They were bold, animating the space around them, and the accessories quivered with colour, more alive than anything she could paint. Next, she drove to a small store ten miles outside Woodstock that sold bric-à-brac masquerading as antiques to choose props for her new school of nudes. Spanish fan with ivory fingers. Riding crop. Glass case of pinned butterflies – tiny Adonis Blue from Europe, Zebra Swallowtail, Smoky Orange Tip from Africa . . . Lastly she bought a fake pistol, a replica of a Mauser.

'Could it be fired?' she asked the sturdy-legged young woman in charge.

'No way,' the woman said, studying Sarah's credit card at different angles.

Sarah put the barrel to her own temple and pulled the trigger. 'Bang.'

'My father taught me never to point a gun at anyone,' the woman said. 'Even a toy.'

Sarah placed the case of butterflies on the passenger seat of the BMW, the rest of her purchases in the back. Driving back to Holyfield, she glanced occasionally at the butterflies and wondered what long-ago lepidopterist had gassed and speared them in the middle of their brief lives. She imagined him brandishing a net, wearing a silly hat, flitting through undergrowth lazy with heat.

In the driving mirror she noticed another car, one hundred yards or so behind her. Green again. The same one? She shrugged it away, noticing at the same time that the butterfly at the top left of the display was a Monarch. Or was it *Hypolimnas misippus*, which had adopted similar colours and markings to the Monarch, orange with black tracings, to fool predators into believing that it *was* the poisonous Monarch.

Harry had taught her everything she knew about butterflies and moths, had lectured her about the Monarch the day she had first suspected that she might be pregnant. 'Lady Monarch lays her eggs on the asclepia plant – orange flowers like her wings. When the eggs become caterpillars they feed off the asclepia which is toxic, hence the Monarch's poison. The caterpillar becomes a chrysalis; ten days later the butterfly emerges from the chrysalis, pumps blood into its wings, dries them and flies away to start the cycle over again.'

The day after the Monarch lecture Dr Storr had said it was highly likely that she was pregnant and arranged for her to go to a lab for blood tests. She decided not to tell Harry until her condition was confirmed. Which it was – the day he disappeared.

She took a bend too fast and the butterfly case slid across the passenger seat. How old were the occupants? she wondered. Exposed to the air, they would crumble like mummies, wing patterns composed of thousands of microscopic and overlapping scales, which would disintegrate into coloured dust.

She had lost the baby – what there was of it, just a blob of protoplasm, but a life just the same – three weeks later, on a Tuesday, when the planets had forecast nothing more untoward than *a shift in your priorities*. Worry, according to Dr Storr, who reminded her of one of those doctors in black and white movies who, bag in hand, emerged from the confinement bedroom shaking their heads ponderously at a distraught husband.

As she braked for the exit from the highway for Holyfield the green car overtook her, the driver hunched over the wheel. She drove slowly through the town, debating whether to stop for lunch, deciding finally to go home, make sandwiches and return to the embryonic painting she had started the previous night. Snow still lay crustily on the fields and to her left the forest was dark by contrast.

As she turned into her drive she picked up fresh tyre marks. Not the BMW's, too thin. She drove the BMW into the garage, warm oil-and-gasolene smell accentuated by the snow, and emerged onto the lawn.

Froze.

The door of the hot-house was wide open and butterflies lay like confetti on the snow.

She ran, slipping wildly, and knelt beside a green Birdwing. A breeze stirred its wings, simulating life, but Sarah knew it was dead.

Warm, jungle-smelling air reached her from the hothouse. She touched the azure wing of Ulysses; blue powder adhered to her finger, and cupped the big inanimate flake that had been *Attacus atlas* in her hand. The false, pink-smeared eyes looked back at her from the tips of the enormous brown wings. One week's life terminated after only two or three days . . .

Screaming soundlessly, she ran into the house. Harris greeted her enthusiastically but she ignored him, picking up the telephone and calling Ben Deacon, only to reach his answering machine. She left a message: 'Please call me. Please.'

She returned to the kitchen and sniffed. There was the faintest fragrance of the cigars Harry had smoked, supposedly rolled in Tampa but, he swore, smuggled into Florida from Cuba. Or was it her imagination? She sniffed again but she was concentrating too hard. She looked for ash and found only crumbs. Imagination. Wasn't it?

She gazed through the window at the bright and fragile lives discarded on the snow.

. . . *culminate with unexpected freedom*. Scarcely ultimate: it was only 2.38. She took a sleeping capsule. Now it would culminate.

She is painting furiously. A mural peopled with nudes, men and women, fornicating, coupling, fucking . . . Ever-inventive man has never come up with an apposite word.

Sarah, lying fully clothed on the couch, smiles. Dusk settles, the breeze stiffens and dead butterflies dance in the snow.

Now she is *in* the painting. No longer a mural, more Botticelli's *The Birth of Venus*. Standing in a shell, one hand to her right breast, coil of long Titian hair pressed to the V of her crotch.

Flowers, daisies, butterflies . . . And the shell is tilted backwards and she is fucking, being fucked, and the phallus is a knife, a gun, a Mauser . . .

Such hackneyed symbolism. Sarah on the couch smiles but there is an erotic curve to the smile. Darkness closes and the dead butterflies skip into it, wings coming to rest on the graves of the Iroquois.

One catches on the peeling bark of a paper birch, *Attacus atlas*. Its wings flap frenetically before the breeze, now a wind, tugs them from the fragile entomological body, devoid as it has been from birth of a proboscis with which to sustain itself, and dispatches them on disparate currents of air. Moonlight alights coldly on field and forest.

Now the phallus is a crucifix.

And she is crying out in orgasm.

But the cries have an orderly rhythm to them, an insistence that is both intrusive and dismissive. Tongue exploring her lips, she reaches for the telephone.

'Hi, it's Ben. What's the problem?'

'The butterflies. They're all dead.'

'I'll be right over,' he says. 'Give me an hour. Don't move.'

'Botticelli. Did you know that was a nickname? It means little barrel.'

Click. Silence.

A thaw developing after dark seemed wrong. Nevertheless she could hear the drip of it outside and it was nearly midnight.

'You're telling me your horoscope forecast what happened to the butterflies?'

'Unexpected freedom . . .'

'For you, not them.'

'They were part of my life.'

Deacon, wearing a fisherman's sweater fuzzed by too much washing, and corduroy slacks, sipped his bourbon and water and rested his elbows on the marble-topped coffee table. 'Are you sure you didn't leave the door of the hot-house open?'

'Are you trying to say I was influenced by the prediction?'

'Did you leave it open?'

'No,' she said, sipping tea. 'Did you smell cigars in the kitchen?'

'Harry's?'

She nodded, fingers picking up warmth from the mug.

'No,' he said. 'Not even contraband Havanas. Did you?'

'I don't know.'

'The smell of Christmas,' he said. 'Very evocative.'

'What am I going to do, Ben?'

'Any minute now, go to bed.'

'With you?'

'To sleep,' he said.

'I don't know . . .'

'I'm *telling* you. I'm your shrink.'

'So what about this stuff about therapist and patient?'

'To sleep,' he said again. 'You and me sharing whatever lies beyond. Odd, isn't it? Husband and wife going to sleep together, lying beside each other, closing their eyes and going their separate ways. Maybe being unfaithful in their dreams, waking, kissing each other: "Love you, honey," and "Me too, sweetheart," when, Christ, what they've just been up to in their sleeping visions! If we could only lie beside each other, touch each other, close our eyes – and meet in that other place.'

'I'm scared, Ben. Really.'

'We'll talk tomorrow. Whatever we do – shrinks, doctors, herbalists – there's nothing we can do that can compare with sleep.'

Her eyelids were weighted by night. 'Sometimes I feel, you know, that the most simple thing would be to join Harry . . . kill myself, no big deal.'

'And let them win?'

'Let who –' eyelids heavy with moonlight, quicksilver, mercury . . .

'Someone's trying to frighten you to death, Sarah,' Ben said. 'We've got to face that. Tomorrow.'

Chapter Ten

A tranquil day possibly interrupted by the appearance of a respected friend . . .

'Me?' Deacon broke an egg into a cup and dropped it, spitting, into boiling sunflower-seed oil.
 'You appeared yesterday.'
 'Your day will be tranquil, anyway.'
 'You're going to make it that way?' Sarah, robed and still damp from the shower, watched another egg splutter.
 'A little therapy. On a full stomach.' He uncurled strips of bacon from a plastic pack.
 'You're doing it the wrong way round,' Sarah said. 'Bacon first, eggs last.'
 'Who said anything about hot eggs?' He turned them in the skillet. 'Doesn't your horoscope say anything about your personal life?'
 'Sometimes. Today,' reading from the forecast, *'don't allow your solitary way of life to affect friendship.'*
 'Like waking up and finding your therapist in bed with you?'
 'Did we meet in our dreams?'
 'I met you. But you can't remember your dream, right?'
 She shook her head and drops of water fell on the table.
 'Because you were drugged. The sleeping capsule . . .'
 He put the eggs in the microwave and consigned the bacon, hissing, to another skillet.
 'Too hot,' Sarah said.

'Oh, boy. The Mrs Beaton of Holyfield.' Deacon, apron printed with flowers of the field over his crumpled shirt, turned the bacon.

They ate hungrily and gulped coffee and the sun illuminated the dripping garden. Outside only a few wings of snow remained and the pigeons had returned to the forest. Sarah began to wonder if she had, in fact, left the door of the hothouse open.

Then they went for a walk. From birch to pine, lay mould deep beneath their feet; centuries of it, Sarah thought, tucking her hand beneath his arm.

'So where were the Indians buried?' he asked.

She pointed to a glade where, despite the weather, the grass was still green, a relic of summer.

'Nothing to mark it?'

'Everyone here knows where it is. It's treated with respect.' She paused. 'Some people reckon they've heard the dead calling.'

'You?'

'I've heard things,' Sarah said. The wind, freshly roused from the direction of the lake, made music in the pines.

'Maybe we should turn back here,' she said.

'The lake?'

'I don't go near it anymore.'

'You should. Face the past and send it packing.'

'Not today,' she said.

'No sweat. *A tranquil day* . . .'

'It will still be frozen. Only a film of ice but, you know, that's even more transparent.' Like a pane of distorting glass.

'Okay,' he said. 'But one day you have to face the lake. Now let's go back and have some therapy.'

With one hand he massaged his scalp beneath his thinning, charcoal black hair. 'Hypnosis is difficult to define.'

'Then don't try,' Sarah said, sitting on the other side of the marble-topped coffee table, watching his other hand talking, wondering what Ambrose Moon would make of it.

'I have to: you've got to understand once again what's happening.'

There was a force within the mind, Deacon said, that could be channelled into therapy. Operations could then be performed painlessly, certain mental conditions cured.

'I have a mental condition?'

'I think you're allowing yourself to be manipulated. And what you've got to do now is rid your mind of all the mumbo-jumbo about hypnotism. Day-dreaming is a form of self-hypnosis. Bible thumpers hypnotize.'

'But we can all resist it?'

'Sure we can. But you don't go to a hypnotist if you don't want to be hypnotized. And you should remember that the best subjects are the intelligent and the sensitive.'

'Flattery will get you everywhere. Who are the most difficult subjects?'

'Hypnotists,' Ben told her. 'Now stand up for a second. Close your eyes. Relax. Completely. Now you're swaying gently from side to side, backwards and forwards. Now open your eyes and stop swaying. The perfect subject, agreeable to suggestion.' he said as she returned to the couch.

'Intelligent and sensitive?'

'I want you to concentrate on what I'm saying.' His brown eyes looked into hers, and beyond. 'You're relaxed . . . you're lying down, sinking down, so relaxed.'

There was a fleck of black in the cornea of one eye close to the pupil. She concentrated on it.

'You're so relaxed you aren't thinking about anything. So relaxed. Asleep, almost, except that you can hear my voice and your limbs are losing their feeling but my voice is still with you . . . my voice . . . carrying you into twilight . . . your breathing is slower, slower . . .'

And now his voice was reaching her in waves from beyond the black fleck in the brown eye. The fleck expanded, obliterating the brown.

'The face in the window . . . That was suggested by your horoscope . . .'

Subject to attentions from a stranger . . .

'A memory of Harry's face beneath the ice . . .'

Her body jolted as though it had been subjected to an electric charge.

'But all that's in the past. Harry is dead and now at long last you are recovering from the loss. You don't need any crutches to help you walk into happiness, no horoscopes . . . The painting of the nude that was slashed – that, too, was suggested by your horoscope . . .'

The dark side of life . . .

'But it did happen,' she tries to say, but the words are pebbles lodged in her mouth.

'. . . and the butterflies escaping . . . That, too, was suggested.' The waves of his voice are stronger now. 'The stars are more remote than the beginning of time and cannot influence us in any way. And you don't want to read their predictions, don't want to need them. Now I will count to six and when I reach six you will open your eyes.'

Two . . . four . . . blackness shrinking . . . five . . . to a speck . . .

'How did we do?' she asked.

'We did just fine.'

'But hypnosis can be dangerous, can't it?'

'In the wrong hands. If, for instance, a post-hypnotic suggestion isn't removed. Supposing a hypnotist suggests that when a white handkerchief is waved you will take three smart steps forward? Supposing you are standing on a cliff top and a total stranger just happens to take a white handkerchief from his pocket?'

'And supposing the cliff is beside a frozen lake?' Sarah said.

'I have reservations about hypnosis too,' Deacon said. 'If a hypnotherapist makes suggestions to a subject and he or she is hostile to them then that hostility will be directed at the hypnotist.'

She sat upright. 'You said last night that someone is trying to frighten me to death.'

'Right. And if I remove your obsession with astrology then I remove their weapon.'

'Then they will find another one!'

'By which time we will have nailed them.'

'We?'

'Us. The police won't do anything.'

'Okay,' Sarah said. 'When do we start?'

'We already have,' Ben said.

He offered to stay another night but she declined the offer; being alone in the house had to be faced.

The tyres of the Cadillac spat gravel as dusk made its way through the forest. At the end of the drive he raised one hand in an Indian salute.

She went into the studio and switched on the light, considered the budding nude on the canvas that she had begun a couple of nights earlier. Even headless it was conventional.

Remembering *Dead Girl*, the sharp-hipped nude in charcoal and water colour by Egon Schiele who had died in 1918, she decided she would resurrect him as her mentor. *Nude Slashed* . . . *Nude with Gun* . . . *Nude under Ice* . . . The possibilities assembled before her, beckoning.

She left the studio, switched out the light and walked towards the homely, herb-smelling kitchen.

There was a whisper of leaves in the birch tree. A silhouette in the dusk. Glint of spectacles. Scarf flapping. Broad brim of a hat angled flamboyantly.

She runs towards it . . . Encounters a birch and, behind it, a tall holly, fading light shining on its polished leaves, a strip of cardboard and a paper tissue lodged in the branches.

She hears a noise like feet sweeping aside leaves on the deep mould. Or is it the wind?

She drinks two Martinis, then a third. Watches television. Takes a sleeping capsule, then a second.

Chapter Eleven

Career trends are positive and the day will be constructive and satisfying . . .

Rebecca Cotton kissed Robbie, smoothed his fine fair hair and handed him over to a beefy cop with a broken-toothed grin named Brennan. Robbie liked him – said his freckles danced – and the feeling seemed to be reciprocated. They entered the elevator discussing Robbie's efforts to hack himself into the Pentagon, failing that the White House. From the window she watched their two diminutive figures climb into the patrol car.

Then she faxed Sarah Logan's prediction – partly hers too. Carman Barea came into the room as it was being transmitted. 'Call for you, Mrs Cotton. Lieutenant Ruben.'

Ruben, whom Rebecca had met, was thin and worried and Jewish. She picked up the phone. 'What can I do for you, lieutenant?'

'A word of advice, Mrs Cotton. It's a week now since we gave Robbie protection. We can't keep it up for ever.'

'How much longer?'

'Until next Monday. If I authorized protection every time a weirdo made a threat in this precinct, there wouldn't be a cop on the streets.'

'But supposing –'

'I know how you feel, Mrs Cotton, believe me. Got kids of my own, boy and a girl.'

'If something happened to Robbie you'd never forgive yourself.'

'Mrs Cotton, every day of my life something happens for which I'll never forgive myself.' Rebecca heard the rustle of paper. 'Here's a guy who can help you. Dave Caffrey – used to be a cop, works for himself these days.' Ruben read out a telephone number. 'Believe me, I'm sorry.'

'I believe you,' Rebecca said.

She met Will in Bryant Park where, on summer evenings, they had once sheltered from the heat and shared the boundless future.

He was standing under a black-fringed sycamore, eating a hot dog and drinking Pepsi from a plastic cup.

'Will Cotton,' she said. 'I always thought it sounded like an old cowboy movie star.'

'Or a character from *Winesburg, Ohio*. How's Robbie?'

'Robbie's okay.' She told him what Ruben had said. 'What do you think?'

'I'll check out Caffrey,' Will said, spectacles glinting wisely. 'Maybe it would be a good idea if Robbie stayed with me. *Us*,' he corrected himself.

'A house is more vulnerable than an apartment and he would have a long journey to school.' She shook her head. 'No, he's safer in the city.'

They began to walk.

'What I don't understand,' Will said, 'is what this guy, this messenger, wants.'

'Maybe nothing. Just another nut.'

'Let's hope so.' They passed an old woman wearing a coat tied with string who was feeding sparrows with cake crumbs. 'One explanation could be your . . . occupation.'

'Call it job if you want.'

'Some of your clients are . . . Give me a word.'

Rebecca gave him: 'Celebrities'.

'You could manipulate them. Had you ever thought about that?'

'Frequently.'

'Law makers, law breakers, politicians, heads of state even.'

'Has it ever occurred to you why movie stars are indisposed on a crucial day of shooting? Why heads of state suddenly send deputies to airports to meet visiting statesmen . . .'

'Not until a couple of minutes ago,' Will said.

'So you figure this – messenger – is going to tell me to manipulate someone?'

'It's the only explanation I can come up with. How's Robbie taking the hassle?'

'Great. He's a star. Who else goes to school in a patrol car?'

'And at night?'

'He's happy enough with his computer, and Fort Knox has nothing on the penthouse,' Rebecca said.

'You're very positive today. Have you prepared your own horoscope?'

'Not exactly,' she said.

'What's that supposed to mean? You said you would never do your own prediction. Too scary.'

'What about this weekend?' Rebecca said. 'I don't think it would be a good idea for Robbie to go to Long Island.'

'I want to see him.'

'The Taurus man loves his kids but he's also sensible about them. Would the witch mind if you stayed in the penthouse?'

Will thought about it, pausing beside a bed of ivy. 'She wouldn't be crazy about it,' he said after a while. 'Matter of fact, she wants me to divorce you.'

'And?'

'I don't know . . . I asked you to marry me right here. Remember?'

'On this corner. Same ivy by the look of it.' She closed her eyes and smelled summer. 'You took your time about it. Taureans usually do.'

'Maybe not long enough. How was I to know that this model with the gorgeous legs was going to become a famous stargazer?'

'Maybe the witch will become a fortune teller.'

They left the park, filtering into the purposeful thrust of 42nd Street.

'So are you going to stay in the apartment over the weekend?' Rebecca said.

Will pinched the bridge of his nose, weighing up the pros and cons like any good lawyer. They stopped in front of a panhandler carrying a placard – I'M BLIND. PLEASE HELP. HAVE A GOOD DAY – and he put a dollar in the beret on the sidewalk beside a scruffy mongrel.

'Well?'

'I'm surprised you asked.'

'I was stupid.'

'We Taureans are methodical but we get there in the end.'

'Robbie is not going to Long Island.'

'He doesn't have to. Make me up a bed in the spare room.' He kissed her on the cheek.

Rebecca smiled fiercely. *Take that, witch! Go fall off your broomstick!*

Sarah circled the fax machine in her study. The horoscope was there waiting for her but she couldn't bring herself to pick it up.

Post-hypnotic suggestion?

What she should have done was fax a cancellation of the whole damn service. But she couldn't face a repetition of last Sunday's withdrawal. Far easier to snatch the prediction from the fax, read it, tear it into scraps and treat its message with cavalier disregard.

She hovered beside the machine hailed as a miracle of communications. But was it really? Surely the transmission of a voice on the phone was more miraculous. Maybe it was an example of regression? Like television. 'Give me a good book any day,' Sarah said aloud.

She stretched her hand but it was heavy and fell to her side. Elastic stretched inside her skull. Hypnosis competed with the stars.

She tried to raise her hand again but it remained inert. She tried the other, willed it to half-mast, but the fingers were curled powerlessly in a claw. Harris howled, his lupine call of the wild.

The phone rang. Deacon – wanting to know if she had read her horoscope.

'You know damn well I haven't.' She heard the snap in her voice.

A sigh. 'I told you this would happen. If a hypnotherapist makes a suggestion to which a subject is hostile, then he becomes the target of the hostility.'

'I want to read the horoscope. Which doesn't mean I'm going to be influenced by it.'

'Very well.' His voice settled professionally. 'Read the horoscope. But remember that your destiny is in your hands – no one else's.'

She cradled the receiver. The elastic snapped in her skull. Her hands felt light as though weights had been removed from them.

She picked up the horoscope.

. . . *constructive and satisfying.*

She relaxed. All she had seen the previous night was a holly bush dressed with cardboard and tissue. The butterflies could be replaced from the store near Pearl Paint. One slashed painting – the world was full of sexually repressed freaks.

What she had to do was paint. But who? She called an amateur model, Pauline Crossley in New Paltz, who had posed for her when Harry was alive. The three of them had become friends: ski-ing in the Adirondacks, disco-ing in New York City.

No reply.

She crossed the spongy lawn to the studio. Behind her the shingled wall of the house steamed in the unexpected sunshine.

The headless nude was still on the easel. She mixed paint and gave it a head. Flaxen hair, cornflower blue eyes . . . Naked, Mary Breeden stared at her reproachfully from the canvas.

Nude with a Gun. She found an uncompleted nude of Pauline Crossley. Lolling indolently, breasts hitched by plastic surgery, black hair drifting across her face, paint warm with her sensuality. Why she had abandoned the painting Sarah couldn't remember.

She replaced Mary Breeden with Pauline on the easel, balanced the replica Mauser against a book, *Degenerate art: The Fate of the Avant-Garde in Nazi Germany*, and began to paint, swiftly and expansively. The gun in Pauline's hand dropped, as though she had just shot someone. Muzzle smoking? No – too obvious. Let's suppose she lost her nerve at the last moment. That the man she was going to kill is still standing in front of her . . .

'Hi,' Sam Parker said from the doorway.

Sarah botched the trigger of the Mauser. Turning, she said: 'Don't ever do that again.'

'Sorry, ma'am. Couldn't help stopping and observing.' He took a step inside the studio. 'Some lady,' nodding at the canvas. 'Do I know her?'

'Not if she saw you first,' Sarah said.

'No need for such hostility. I'm here to help you, Mrs Logan.' He nodded towards the Mauser replica. 'You got a licence for that?'

'You know it's a fake as well as I do.'

'Lots of heists have been pulled with fake guns. Why's the lady holding the gun, Mrs Logan?'

'I'm sure you'll make your own interpretations.'

'Looks kind of . . . suggestive to me.'

Sarah began to paint again, brush following the barrel of the pistol.

Parker folded his arms. He was wearing a green and mauve track suit and running shoes and there was a sheen of sweat on his face.

He pointed at *Nude Slashed*. 'Jesus,' he said. He noticed Mary Breeden and laughed.

'Don't let me keep you,' Sarah said.

'I was thinking about that conversation we had. You know, about painting male nudes instead of female. Seems kind of unnatural to me, a woman painting naked women.'

Sarah added the front sight to the barrel of the Mauser.

'I'm getting old,' Parker said.

'Old?'

'And forgetful.'

'I don't know what the hell you're talking about, Officer Parker.'

'Forgot to send those prints to Albany.'

'That was more than forgetful,' Sarah said. 'That was negligent.'

'I can still send them.'

'Do it.'

'Like I told you, I checked them out.'

'Nothing positive . . . you said something like that.'

'Not much doubt though. Not in my mind. Your prints check with the handle of the knife and the knife was yours.'

Sarah stood back and surveyed the painting. 'Just what are you getting at, Officer Parker?'

'It would be a crying shame if it got around town. Sarah Logan slashed her own painting . . .'

'You mean you want to pose for me?'

'Ain't nothing wrong with the male body. Not if it's looked after.'

'And if I paint you then no one gets to know about the matching prints?'

'You got it,' Parker said.

'Okay. Strip.'

His body was lithe, evenly tanned as though he used a sun lamp. He was pulling in his belly a little but making no attempt to cover his erection.

Sarah began to mix paints.

'How do you want me?'

'Kneeling for a sprint, throwing an imaginary discus . . . However you see yourself.'

She added red and yellow to the mix.

'Like this, I guess.' He sat on the couch, crossed his legs and stared at Pauline Crossley holding the Mauser. 'How's this?'

'Fine,' Sarah said. 'That's just fine.'

She scooped the paint mix into a bowl and added water and a blob of Prussian blue.

'First male nude you've painted, I guess.'

'The very first,' Sarah said. 'You're very . . . virile Officer Parker.'

'Call me Sam. You're an exciting woman, Sarah. But I guess you can see how you affect me.'

'A compliment, believe me.' She moved closer to the couch. 'Maybe I'll call the picture *Macho in Ascent*. Or maybe *in Descent*,' pouring the contents of the bowl over his crotch.

Chapter Twelve

A productive and pleasurable period with Venus in your solar ninth house. Accept advice from business partners but be particularly protective with children or surrogates...

Well, she hadn't got any children – a momentary emptiness inside her – and no surrogates, so this was the third rosy prediction in a row

She finished *Nude with a Gun*, added a butterfly to the pattern of the couch and stood it beside *Nude Slashed* and Mary Breeden in the flesh. What next? She picked up the riding crop she had bought in the store near Woodstock and called Pauline Crossley again. No reply. Janice Gotthardt? She compressed her lips. So who? A professional model? She shook her head: she preferred amateurs because they looked vulnerable.

Mary Breeden? She giggled.

She found another painting of Pauline Crossley and placed it on the easel. Flexed the crop, imagined it held between Pauline's hands, laid it on the couch, and began to paint. Carefully, because she didn't want to over emphasise any suggestion of sadism, although of course the picture would exude sexuality.

The phone rang.

'So how are the exhibits coming along?' Mike Kaplan asked.

'I've done some things which I think will interest you,' Sarah told him.

'What kind of things?'

'Come and see for yourself.'

'Matter of fact, I was driving up anyway. I want to discuss the advertising with you.'

'You meant you want me to pay for it?'

'Now come on,' he said. 'What do you think this is, a vanity gallery?'

'Any more definite don't knows for the opening? Milton Esterow, Elizabeth Baker, Donald Kuspit . . ?' *Fat chance*, she thought.

'Interest is hotting up,' Kaplan said. 'What we need is a gimmick.'

'Maybe I've got one,' Sarah said, looking at the painted slashes on Janice Gotthardt's groin.

'Great. How about four this afternoon?'

'Four would be fine,' Sarah said, dipping her brush into a mix the colour of old ivory for the handle of the crop.

When she had finished her stint she walked into Holyfield, making a diversion to the ground where a game of lacrosse was in progress: a team from Montreal versus Holyfield. Mary Breeden was watching it, with Josephine Mowat – the woman who was writing a thesis on the victims of rape – standing beside her.

Mary Breeden greeted her convivially. 'A rugged game, Sarah. Ever thought of taking it up?'

'Painting is rugged enough for me,' she said.

'The Indians called it Baggataway. The evening before a game they called on the Great Spirit for Victory. Medicine men were umpires . . .'

'How's the painting going?' asked Josephine Mowat, an intense and darkly handsome woman who licked every word into shape before issuing it.

'Couldn't be better,' Sarah said.

The two teams were passing the ball from the nets on their sticks with the ferocity of prize fighters.

'Aren't you encouraging sexual fantasies?'

'Aren't fantasies preferable to reality?'

'One thing leads to another,' Josephine Mowat said.

'Sometimes a game ended in death,' Mary Breeden said. 'Or slaughter. In 1763 George III's birthday was celebrated by a game at Fort Michillmackmac, a British garrison. The

Ottawas, led by their chief, Pontiac, laid on a game against the Ojibways outside the fort. When the British soldiers came out to watch, the Indians picked up tomahawks instead of sticks and killed them all.'

'The British,' Josephine Mowat said, 'must have been very naive.'

'And very dead,' said Sarah.

'The Canadians play it indoors,' Mary Breeden said. 'They call it box lacrosse.'

'In Britain it's the women's game that has developed,' Josephine Mowat said. 'No bodily contact allowed, but pretty vicious just the same.' She winced as a Canadian scooped the ball off the ground and sent it hurtling to a colleague. 'But it's all good, healthy fun.'

'Unlike painting nudes?'

'Depends on the kind of nudes. I hear some of yours are kind of weird.'

'Officer Parker told you that?'

'A painting of a nude slashed *is* kind of weird. You don't think that encourages perverts?'

'What encourages perverts,' Sarah said, 'is repression. Victorian hypocrisy. Papa kissing the kids goodnight and saving the souls of a few hookers before screwing the maid by gaslight.'

'Holyfield is a decent town,' Mary Breeden said. 'We're decent people and we want to keep it that way.'

'Is this a last warning?'

'Interpret it whatever way you want.'

One of the players blocked an opponent who fell squirming to the ground.

Sarah said: 'I've been reading up lacrosse in the library. Queen Victoria watched a game between Canadians and Iroquois at Windsor Castle in 1876. Know what she said?' And before Mary Breeden could reply: 'She said it was "very pretty to watch".'

In the grocery store Sarah shopped wildly: Aunt Jemima's original waffles, Heavenly Hash ice-cream, Californian sun-dried Calimyrna figs, Seven Seas Green Goddess dressing, cold meats, cartons of frozen pink lemonade . . . She hadn't drunk that since she was a kid.

In the square she saw Sam Parker, thumbs in the belt of his uniform. He ignored her, so she had achieved something.

In Noveck's she ordered a milkshake, chocolate this time, and joined Ambrose Moon at his observation post.

'You've sure shed a load of worry,' he said, feeling the long fingers of one hand as though they were pencils.

'The shoulders?'

'Dropped nicely. And your gestures – very bold. Stars been kind to you, Mrs Logan?'

'How do you know about the stars?'

'I don't. But most women follow them, don't they? First item they read in the newspapers, magazines. Men just *happen* to glance at them . . . You do read yours, don't you, Mrs Logan?'

'If I said no my leg would start to swing.'

'Which it isn't. Another reprieve, Mrs Logan?'

She pulled one ear, tapped the side of her nose, put her finger to her lips.

'The works,' Ambrose Moon said. 'But I was looking at your left hand. It's fisted. That's no way to drink a milkshake.'

She walked home, swinging her bag of goodies, and let Harris out of the kitchen giving him the don't-go-too-far lecture. As usual he galloped into the forest, clown's ears – one black, one white – streaming.

She made herself an exotic salad and drank pink lemonade. Outside the miraculous sunshine delivered messages from childhood: flying a Chinese kite in Maine, to where they had moved from New Jersey, watched dutifully by her parents; Sunday brunch when guests asked her dumb questions and her parents answered for her; a diploma for art while her parents applauded grimly; and the escape hatches – a poppy field where red petals crinkled like moths in the breeze, a barn furnished with bales of straw which could be shifted to build miniature rooms and corridors.

The trouble with childhood loneliness was that you didn't recognize it for what it was: the result of circumstance. Instead you observed other children who enjoyed friendships generated by family warmth, and envied them. Not that her mother and father had been uncaring but each had been a dictionary parent – *one who has begotten or borne offspring.*

Harris trotted across the lawn, less exuberantly than usual, and pawed the kitchen door. She let him in and he subsided in his basket, nose between his paws.

Mike Kaplan, who was never late, arrived at four, glossy and alert, dressed in denim. She showed him her latest paintings.

'Jesus Christ, what's that supposed to be? Disgusted of Guttenberg getting out of the tub?' He peered closer. 'She isn't even a natural blonde.'

'*The Enemy Without*,' Sarah said. *Mary Breeden.*

'Without clothes, sure. Without depth, too. Without character . . . You're putting me on, aren't you, Sarah? Please say yes.'

She showed him *Nude with a Gun*. 'Oh boy,' he said. She heard his breathing quicken as, finger and thumb to his jaw, he contemplated Pauline Crossley. Then: 'Wow, now we really have something for the gangland-slaying media. If you've got some more like that . . .'

She showed him *Nude Slashed*. That, too, silenced him. Until: 'That's just about the most obscenely beautiful thing I've ever seen.' He did a mock shudder. 'Who is the unfortunate lady?'

'Her name is Janice Gotthardt.'

'She lives here?'

'Near the sawmill.'

'Great! I'll arrange interviews.'

'I don't think her husband would like that.'

'For a small fee?'

'He'd adore it,' Sarah said.

Mike Kaplan rubbed his smooth, manicured fingers together. 'Anything more? We could be starting a new school of painting here.'

Pauline Crossley holding the riding crop.

He whistled. 'Think of the outrage we can generate!'

'We've already got it,' Sarah said. 'But I don't want to get a reputation as a pornographic artist. That wasn't the idea: I wanted to catch the positive sensuality that so many women possess – beneath the camouflage.'

'Camouflage?'

'Being good mothers and wives. Picking up the kids. Packing for vacations. Charming the breadwinner's clients. Arranging flowers. Meeting for coffee . . .'

'*Nude Slashed* expresses all that?'

'That's the source of it: a vulnerable woman attacked. From that stems *Nude with a Gun* etcetera. Women on the attack, asserting their desires.'

'I like it,' said Mike. 'I really do. How about *Nude Observed*? You know, the peeper. How many can you do before the exhibition?'

'Maybe half a dozen, give or take. I'm painting faster these days.'

'I wanted to talk about advertising but that's all changed now. I can see the catalogue . . .'

He fetched a Polaroid camera from his Porsche and took some shots. 'I'll send up a pro. Meanwhile don't let that brush out of your fingers.' He touched the pistol in Pauline Crossley's hand. 'How about a dribble of smoke?'

'I don't think so,' Sarah said.

Harris began to convulse at 6.35.

Sarah stroked him, looked into his frightened eyes and called the vet.

The vet, middle-aged with a monkish fringe of hair, knelt, stared into Harris's mouth and eyes, felt his muscles, took his temperature. Rocking back on his heels, he said: 'He's got a fever and he's having difficulty in breathing. If I were a physician . . .'

Harris convulsed again, legs jerking in a series of spasms. When they had passed he lay still in his basket gazing reproachfully at Sarah.

'If you were a physician, what?'

'Has he been out today?'

'He had a run in the forest.'

'You see, I figure he's been poisoned. And if I were a physician . . . Does anyone sniff coke here?'

'No one,' Sarah said.

'I would diagnose cocaine poisoning.'

'That's ridiculous,' Sarah said.

'Maybe, but he's got all the symptoms. Have you had a fight with anyone about Harris? Has he bitten anyone, molested them?'

'No one. And if anyone wanted to poison him they surely wouldn't use cocaine.'

'They just might,' the vet said, standing up. 'If they were hooked on it themselves and had a good supply. That way there would be no trace of them buying poison.'

'Why would anyone want to poison Harris?'

The vet checked his fringe with one hand. 'It happens, Mrs Logan. It happens. To you he's a friend. Maybe to someone else he's a pest.'

'He'll be okay, won't he?'

Harris closed his eyes, one black ear covering the side of his face.

'I'll take a chance,' the vet said, taking a hypodermic and an ampoule from his bag. 'The best treatment for cocaine poisoning is a quick-acting barbiturate. It relieves the depression of the central nervous system that causes respiratory collapse.' The needle slid into a patch of white fur.

'Nothing more I can do,' the vet said. 'Give me a call in a couple of hours.'

'You can't be dying,' Sarah said when the vet had left. 'Not you.' She arranged the black ear for him. He opened his eyes and, she thought, recognized her. He wagged his tail twice.

He died at 7.28.

Surrogate?

Rebecca Cotton called Mrs Skipton early to check that Robbie was safely installed in school. He was just fine, Mrs Skipton said wearily; sitting at his desk studying mathematics, his best subject.

'He's going to be a computer whizz,' Rebecca said.

'By the time he's grown up,' Mrs Skipton said, 'we won't need brains any more.'

Rebecca checked with Lieutenant Ruben to make sure that Brennan would pick him up from school and telephoned Will who was at home that day, a Friday.

The witch took the call. 'Will tells me you want him to stay with you over the weekend.' Even her voice sounded plump.

'I'm worried about Robbie and I figured it would be safer for him to stay in the apartment.'

'In big, bad New York city? Surely he would be safer here.'

'I don't think so. He *is* my son. And Will's,' Sarah added.

'Don't you think you're paying too much attention to a threat from some nut?'

'A risk I don't care to take, Mrs Wessel. Can I speak with my husband, please?'

'He told you about filing for divorce?'

'He told me you wanted him to get one.'

'And he said –'

A click. Will's voice on an extension: 'I'll take this, Beth.'

'– he would see his lawyer?'

'He is a lawyer,' Rebecca said. 'Or haven't you got that far in his CV?'

'I've checked out Caffrey and he's picking Robbie up on Monday – if that's what you're calling about,' Will said.

'Can you make it tonight, Will? I'd feel happier.'

A pause. 'Did the stars tell you to say that?'

'I'd just feel happier.'

Another click. Beth Wessel had picked up the main receiver again.

'We were going out to dinner,' Will said.

'Which is more important, dinner or your son?'

'Don't put me on the spot, Rebecca. That's an unfair question – no judge would allow it.'

'Do I hear the jury on the other line?'

'Will hasn't even made up his mind whether he's going to your apartment on Saturday,' Beth Wessel said.

'But I thought –'

'Let Will do the thinking.'

'Will?'

'I'll get back to you.'

Rebecca put down the receiver. Craven coward. Methodical Taurean wimp.

The phone rang. 'Expect me at seven,' Will said. 'Traffic permitting.'

Rebecca almost felt sorry for the witch. But not quite.

Chapter Thirteen

. . . trouble with communications.

Sarah awoke from tangled dreams driven by dark resolve: the death of Harris had to be avenged.

Her mood was assisted by the day. Winter had snapped its jaws overnight and the grey sky ached with cold. She showered and dressed and made coffee, feeling bereft without Harris, utterly alone.

She dug a grave among the birch trees and laid his body in it. She adjusted the black ear into decent repose and shovelled earth over him. There were no flowers left in the garden but she hammered together a temporary cross from a picture frame and stuck it in the earth. She stood for a moment beside the grave. What was it Ben had said? '*By which time we will have nailed them.*' Now all that had changed. Now it was *her* fight.

She read her horoscope defiantly – no need because the predictions were relatively trivial – dressed for town and drove across the Hudson to Poughkeepsie where she boarded a New York-bound train. Staring across the sullen waters of the river towards West Point, she reflected that, in reverse, this was part of the last journey Harry had made. On the day he disappeared. The day he died. What had he been thinking?

The train passed through Ossining Correctional Facility, better known as Sing Sing, then Tarrytown and Irvington, near the home of Rip Van Winkle's creator Washington Irving.

She felt that the train was burrowing back into Harry's life. Had he at this stage of the journey had any presentiment that he was going to die? Had his death really been accidental? Yonkers, Spuyten Duyvil, Marble Hill, a desolate glimpse of Harlem . . . Then the train charged the three-mile long tunnel leading to Grand Central.

From the station she took a cab to Ben Deacon's apartment and consulting rooms. It was Saturday so hopefully he wouldn't be working.

He greeted her wearing an old fawn cardigan and grey slacks, looking like a hawk sheltering from the elements. He made coffee, and in the expensively untidy living room with a squeezed view of the East River she told him about Harris.

'Was it predicted?'

She explained about the warning. 'I guess I shouldn't have let him run in the forest.'

'Bullshit! The horoscope had nothing to do with his death. Coincidences happen to everyone every day of their lives, but you've become obsessed with them.'

'You said someone was trying to scare me to death.'

'Damn right. The peeper, the slashed painting, the butterflies, now Harris . . . Why don't you come and stay here?'

Sarah wagged one finger from side to side. *Ambrose Moon, what do you make of that*? 'I've got to see this through by myself, otherwise it's defeat. That's what I came to tell you: this is my fight.'

'Every fighter needs a second. I've been making inquiries.'

'And?'

'When I come up with something positive, I'll let you know.'

'Okay,' Sarah said, sipping instant coffee. 'So I'll accept help from my second.' And she told him about the green automobile that might have been following her when she drove to Woodstock. 'Can you help me trace it?'

'If you've got the number of the licence plate.'

'That's the point,' Sarah said. 'I don't. But I thought that if –'

'I regressed you?'

'Is it possible?'

'It might be if you sub-consciously noted it. It wouldn't be strictly regression – you'd be in a state of hypermnesis, increased memory. Did you see the driver?'

'Male, I think, but I'm not sure. He was hunched over the wheel. If I noted anything else I forgot it when I found the butterflies in the snow.'

'Okay,' he said. 'Come into the consulting room and relax on the couch. Just like the old days.'

The wooded slopes of the Catskills were tiger-striped with sunlight; the green automobile was behind the BMW.

'You see it in the driving mirror. In a frame. It registers in your mind. What make of car?'

'A Dodge maybe. Or a Chev, Toyota . . . I only caught a glimpse.'

The gallery in Woodstock, walls hung with intimidating virgins.

'And now you're leaving, glancing in the frame of the driving mirror. You see the green car?'

'No. I see a truck delivering Budweiser and a motorcyclist wearing a helmet.'

The bric-a-brac store. Riding crop, preserved butterflies, Mauser . . . Bang, you're dead.

'And you're on your way once again. In the frame of the mirror . . .'

'A green automobile.'

'Same one?'

'I don't know.'

'Make?'

'Could be almost anything.'

'Licence number. You can see it there in the mirror. The plate. It prints itself in your mind . . . The state . . .'

'White background. Navy lettering. Red line on top and bottom. Red fuzz in between the letters and numbers, three on either side.'

'Red fuzz? It's clearer than that.'

'Arm raised. The Statue of Liberty.'

'New York. Terrific. It's been there all the time. Like the number. The number . . .'

'A one and a three. And an E. And a couple of sevens.'

'Let them rearrange themselves in the driving mirror, in the mirror of your mind.'

The BMW takes a corner. The driving mirror is blank.

'No sweat. You're approaching Holyfield and you're going to take an exit. Then the green auto overtakes you and there is the rear licence plate in front of you. Read it out.'

'A two and a one and an E . . . or vice versa . . . the Statue of Liberty . . . sevens and a three . . . Anyway, there is an E, and sevens, probably two of them, and a one and a two . . .

Main Street, Holyfield. Butterflies on the snow.

'I flunked, didn't I?' Sarah said as Deacon snapped his fingers.

'Not completely. We've got a permutation we can work on. I'll feed it to the cops – I've done a lot of work for them. But there is a snag.'

'A snag?'

'They think all hypnotherapists are crazies.'

From Ben Deacon's apartment Sarah walked three blocks to Rebecca Cotton's.

Christmas tree lights flickered on-off in the windows of restaurants, a roaming red-nosed Santa Claus nipped from a bottle of Wild Turkey which he produced from beneath his beard. Cold breathed down the street from the East River.

Nodding at the doorman in the maroon uniform, she walked into the lobby and asked the receptionist at the half-moon desk planted on a chipped marble floor if she could speak to Rebecca Cotton.

The receptionist, who looked like Mike Tyson, buzzed her apartment and said: 'Take a seat. A man is coming down to see you.'

The man was tall, wearing a brown blazer and, with his spectacles, looked like a lawyer, although possibly he wasn't.

'My name's Will Cotton. What can I do for you?'

'I want to see Athena – Rebecca Cotton. Are you her husband?'

'Are you a client?'

Sarah said she was and Will Cotton said: 'She doesn't see clients in person, you must know that.'

'This is important.'

'It always is. You want to know how you can cope with your prediction?'

'More than that, Mr Cotton. I want to know why I'm being manipulated.'

'I can tell you that, Mrs –'
'Logan.'
'It's because you're manipulating yourself. *Allowing* the stars, the planets, to guide you.'
'You don't sound like a believer.'
'I neither believe nor disbelieve, Mrs Logan. That's the only way in most things in this life.'
'Are you a lawyer?'
'I don't practise,' he said, fingering the brass buttons on his blazer as though they were knobs on a radio.
'You teach?'
'Columbia,' he said. 'How are you being manipulated?'
Peepers, slashers, releasers of butterflies, dog poisoners . . .
'It doesn't matter,' she said. 'Just believe me.'
'I'll give her your message. Maybe Monday . . .'
'Why not today?'
'She isn't in the apartment right now.'
'I can wait.'
'I'm sorry, Mrs Logan. You see, in a way we're being manipulated too. Call her Monday.' He walked towards the elevator, footsteps as slow as the due processes of the law.

Emerging on Fifth Avenue, Sarah joined frozen-faced Christmas shoppers foraging for gifts and, by the look of them, good cheer. Plastic in hand, she made hasty purchases in illustrious emporiums: Gucci loafers for Mike Kaplan, computer chess for Ben, sexy lingerie for Janice Gotthardt . . . A genital pouch for Sam Parker? No simulated bones this year for Harris.

Then she boarded a train at Grand Central. Dusk was settling over the Hudson and she tried to pick up the discarded thoughts of Harry as the train neared Poughkeepsie. Her BMW was waiting for her as patiently as an unanswered telephone, close to the space where Harry had settled into a cab.

When she got home the phone was ringing.

She plucked the receiver from the wall in the kitchen and said: 'Hallo,' instead of reciting the number as her mother had taught her.

A breathy silence. She reached with the back of her hand for Harris. Beyond the table stood his basket, empty and gnawed.

'Hallo, who is it?'

. . . trouble with communications.

The concentration of silence intensified.

'If there's anyone there speak up.'

What they told you was: hang up.

Knuckles bone-white, she edged the receiver towards the wall set. Then came a wispy voice, words unintelligible.

'Speak up. Are you scared to identify yourself?'

'Wrong. It is you who is scared.'

The scraped voice was faintly familiar. The previous call? *'You next'*? The curtains moved and the square of light on the frozen lawn trembled.

'Fuck you, mister,' Sarah said. 'Why should I be scared by an impotent phone creep?'

'But you are scared, Sarah.' *Cradle the receiver*: 'Aren't you?'

No.

'Aren't you?'

'What do you want?'

'The usual message, Sarah – you next.'

'Fuck you.'

'Later, Sarah. Later tonight, huh?'

'I –'

Click.

She called emergency.

A bored woman's voice answered. 'What exactly was the threat?'

Sarah told her.

'Okay, so give me your details, name, address . . .'

Sarah gave them. 'He told me he was going to call again tonight. Can you monitor all calls to me?'

'We'll see what we can do, Mrs Logan. But, you know, obscene calls aren't all that uncommon. If they persist we suggest you change your number.'

'This wasn't obscene,' Sarah said.

'No, well . . .' A yawn expanded her voice.

'So you'll do it?'
'We'll be in touch.'

Twenty minutes later the phone rang again. *Leave it*! And again. Mouth dry, she picked up the receiver. 'Who is it?'

It was Sam Parker. 'Telephone people tell me you're getting threatening phone calls.'

Parker's voice calmed her. All that watery paint dripping down his bare legs . . .

'Just another pervert,' she said. 'Don't give it another thought.'

'You seem to attract perverts, Mrs Logan.'

'That's right,' she said, 'I do. I usually throw paint at them.'

She made herself a Martini and found a movie on TV, a police procedural with two cops who joshed each other a lot and said shit every time the bad guys won a point. Harry had once counted twenty three shits and eight sonofabitches in just such a film.

Fifteen minutes later the phone rang again.

'Shit,' said one of the cops.

Ignore it!

It stopped ringing. Five minutes later it started again. Supposing it was her mother calling to say her father had suffered a heart attack? Ben calling to say he had a lead? *Pick it up and leave it off the hook*.

'Sonofabitch,' said the other cop.

She took the call in her study. The wispy voice was hurried this time. 'You next.' And before she could react *he* had hung up. She stared at the receiver in her hand, cradled it. For all she knew he could be calling from Seattle.

It rang again almost immediately. Had they traced the call? The voice of the woman on emergency, not quite so bored this time. 'We've got the number from which the call was made.' A pause. 'Does this number mean anything to you?' She read out the digits.

'Oh yes,' Sarah said, holding the receiver away from her and staring at it. 'It means something all right. You see, I've got two numbers – and that's one of them.'

She reached the kitchen as the light in the studio went out.

Chapter Fourteen

A contradictory day in which uncertainty of purpose is interwoven with recollections of domestic security . . .

Rebecca transmitted the horoscopes, Sarah Logan's included, early. When Carmen Barea, who normally faxed the predictions on Sunday mornings, reported for work at 7 a.m. all that was left for her to do was seal a week's predictions in envelopes for those faxless clients for dispatch by courier service the following morning. She had left by 9 a.m. leaving the apartment to the three of them: Robbie still asleep in his room papered with posters of basketball stars, Will in the inhospitable guest room stacked with the memorabilia of their lives together.

She poured orange juice from a carton into three glasses and began to worry that the long weekend might not have been such a good idea for Robbie, recreating family togetherness which wouldn't be prolonged. Unless . . .

Will came into the gadget-filled kitchen wearing a blue bath robe which she didn't remember, yawning and stretching elaborately. He gulped his juice and stared down into the deserted street where a plume of steam issued from the bowels of the city.

'More snow?' He stretched again and a bone cracked faintly. 'Getting old,' he said, rubbing his shoulder. 'But we all are, aren't we, from the moment we're born?' He sat at the table toying with the cutlery on the eggshell-blue surface. Once he had absent-mindedly bent forks and she had bought plastic cutlery to deter him.

She fetched a pack of cereal from a cupboard, sprinkled it in two dishes and poured milk on it. It crackled with good health.

'So what are we going to do?' he asked, spooning cereal.

'About what?'

'We can't go on like this. With Robbie, that is. We can't keep him prisoner.'

'Today,' she said, 'we can hang the Christmas decorations. Like we used to. Same old tacky fairy on top of the tree.'

'He's got to get out. Got to breathe, Okay, Caffrey's picking him up tomorrow – but what about weekends, vacations? He finishes school for Christmas this week.'

'We can't risk his life.' She remembered the knife in the hand of the man with the poet's face.

'We'll give it to the end of the year.'

'Longer,' Rebecca said. 'We can afford it.'

'*You* can afford it.'

'Cut down on the witch's housekeeping!'

'Let's not fight,' he said, and began to eat his cereal.

'Here's a suggestion,' said Rebecca, sitting opposite him. 'Why don't we call Caffrey and ask him to start today? Then we could go for a walk in Central Park, like we used to.'

'With a shadow?' Will stared at a spoonful of nutritious sludge. 'Okay. Why not?'

Caffrey arrived at eleven, a big square man with pale hair and keyboard teeth. Robbie greeted him guardedly. 'Are you into computers?'

'No,' Caffrey said, 'but I'd like to learn. Can you teach me?'

'Brennan didn't need any teaching,' Robbie said.

'Ah. Brennan.'

'Do you carry a gun?'

Caffrey patted his grey topcoat on the left side. 'Smith & Wesson.'

'Brennan had a Magnum. He said it could blow your head off."

'Robbie!' Rebecca's hand went to her mouth.

'Brennan thinks he's Clint Eastwood,' Caffrey said.

'How can you get your gun out if your coat's buttoned?'

'I unbutton it,' Caffrey said. 'Why don't you show me your computer?'

'You really want to see it?'

'Know what I'd really like? I'd like to learn how to hack into the FBI headquarters.'

'Nothing to it,' Robbie said, and led the way into his room.

'They'll be okay,' Will said.

'But will *we* be okay?' Sarah asked.

'Like I said, it's worse at Christmas.'

'Have you made up your mind where you're going to spend Christmas Day?'

'Beth's being decent about it. She suggested half the day with her, half with you and Robbie.'

'She's a decent woman,' Rebecca said. 'Dragging you away from your son on Christmas Day – that's what I call decency with a capital SH.'

'No,' Will said, 'she wouldn't be dragging me away. I'd come after lunch and stay.'

'After the presents have been opened? After the turkey and the plum pudding? . . . I'm sorry,' she said, 'she's a witch and I'm a bitch.'

'This apartment . . . it isn't exactly Christmassy.'

'We could have had a place in the country as well.'

'With your money, anything's possible.'

'With our joint incomes.' She hoped she wouldn't cry. 'Remember the modern version of charades in the evening?'

'*The Bible.* Bye – waving like crazy. Bull – charging head down.'

Rebecca laughed, which was convenient because it disguised the fact that she was also crying. She went to the bathroom to repair her face, then to her bedroom where she dressed in slacks and jersey and put on a long black coat. When she returned to the kitchen, Will said: 'I keep imagining Robbie waking on Christmas morning and finding me not here.'

They entered the park through the Artists' Gate and walked round the pond, Caffrey following twenty-five yards or so behind them, surprisingly inconspicuous despite his square bulk. From the pond they struck out to the Mall, with its elm trees and busts of the famous. Joggers panted past them like survivors in the desert sighting a mirage; cyclists overtook the joggers with patronizing dignity.

'Did you know that women cyclists here were once denounced because they showed a bit of leg?' Rebecca said.

'Marie Dressler used to cycle here,' Will said. 'Lillian Russell, too, on a gold-plated bike.'

Robbie ran ahead, breath smoking on the cold air. Rebecca glanced behind: Caffrey was still there, a sturdy chameleon. But Robbie was too far ahead now – anyone could snatch him – and Rebecca called to him to come back.

When he returned Will told him about the park: that during the Depression in the thirties the hungry and homeless had camped here and a shanty town had grown up in the empty reservoir.

'I know,' Robbie said. 'And they ate all the ducks and fish in the lake.'

They reached the Bethesda Fountain and the lake and made their way to the statue of Hans Christian Andersen and, nearby, Alice in Wonderland and acquaintances on a toadstool.

'It's a conspiracy,' Will said. 'Christmas, Hans Andersen, Alice . . .'

'It's a children's time. A parents' time, too. Robbie feels that, I guess, without actually recognizing it. That's why he's a smart-ass when you're around: he's being defiant.'

Will took her arm and they left the park at 72nd Street, children's playground to their right.

After lunch they decorated the tree, Robbie in charge of the lower boughs, Will the upper branches and the lights which predictably didn't work and took half an hour to fix, Rebecca in overall command with special responsibility for the deployment of angel hair and tinsel. The result was a mix of Manhattan chic and folksy.

At 8.30 Will announced, with rehearsed casualness, that it was time for him to leave. Rebecca waited for Robbie to ask why but instead he ran to his room, slamming the door behind him.

Will glanced at Rebecca. 'Aren't you going to say goodbye?' he called.

'Goodbye, Dad.' Came a muffled voice.

'I'll go to him,' Will said.

'No, leave him.'

'I'll think about Christmas Day.'

'Don't torture yourself. Spend the whole day with the witch if that's what you really want.'

He wiped his spectacles with a handkerchief. 'I'm sorry.' He put on his topcoat, hesitated at the door, shook his head, frowned, and went out, closing the door gently behind him.

Rebecca went back into the living-room and sat in front of the Christmas tree. After a while she leaned forward, rearranging a lock of angels' hair.

There was the faintest fragrance of cigar smoke in the studio. Could anything more pungently evoke *recollections of domestic security*?

And a *contradictory day*. No kidding – nothing more contradictory than the worshipful quiet of a Sunday morning after a night locked in a creaking house, the owner of the you-next voice possibly prowling the grounds, trying the doors, breathing wispily. . . .

Sarah closes the door of the studio to keep out the quiet: she took two sleeping capsules at 5.35 a.m. and at midday her senses are still drugged. She hears the colours of the paint – red growls and yellow chimes – and smells the incense odour of church bells.

She paints wildly, raucous gashes of acrylic. What was it Mike Kaplan had suggested? *Nude Observed*? Well, she'd give the peeper something to observe. She paints herself. Naked – although she doesn't strip – as seen through steamed-up glass. Swollen nipples, shaven crotch.

She searches for a prop. The Mauser replica. Mouth open, she aims the barrel at her open mouth, licks her lips, tightens her finger on the trigger.

Smiles, senses beginning to normalize. Points the barrel at the skylight. Pulls the trigger. The bullet punches out the glass and despite the smothering roar of the shot she hears the tinkle of the shards as they fall melodiously around her.

Chapter Fifteen

Be prepared for a rapid-fire sequence of events that may soon lead to a radical change in your life.

She would not allow herself to be manipulated by the forecast. And she would continue to fight the *unseen enemies* of her general horoscope.

She took the forecast from the fax machine without difficulty, the post-hypnotic suggestion implanted by Ben Deacon having been removed. If someone was trying to frighten you to death hypnosis wasn't the antidote – it merely lulled you into a false sense of security – and Sarah resented Ben's presumption.

She took the sheet of slippery paper into the kitchen and struck a match. Then blew it out: to burn the prophecy was to admit its strength. Instead she placed it on the table beside one of her unrequited lists of tasks. Mug of coffee in front of her, she began another list – a campaign plan.
(1) *Confront Athena, Rebecca Cotton, and question the source of her prophecies which are so uncannily accurate.*
(2) *Check with Ben to see if he's traced the licence plate of the green car.*
(3) *Trace ownership of the genuine Mauser pistol which was substituted for the replica.*
(4) *Ensure that all telephone calls are monitored.*
(5) *Monitor yourself, kid – go confront the lake.*

She swallowed the last of the coffee which was now tepid and reflected that, despite everything, she felt surprisingly alert – good night's sleep in the warm burrow of her bed, no sleeping capsule to dull perception. She showered, dressed and went to the studio, hub of the enemy's campaign. Peeper, slashing of the painting, phone call, substitution of loaded pistol for fake . . .

She picked up the pistol and, very professionally, checked the remaining bullets, just as the joshing cops on the TV serial would have done. Five left. The first would have blown out her brains if she had fired it into the roof of her mouth – or into her temple, the way she had pretended to do in the store near Woodstock.

She took a pair of shears from the garden shed, blades steel bright and greased, and clipped a few shrubs because gardening soothed her. The branches and twigs were bone bare, earth frozenly obdurate beneath. The cold burned her ears, made her eyes water. The lake would be frozen now, groaning with its burden.

She dropped the shears so that they stayed upright, tips of the blades supported by the hard soil, and walked past the deserted hot-house, deciding as she went to buy more eggs and pupae from the store on the Lower West Side.

Making her way through the forest, missing the snuffling explorations of Harris, she listened to the voices reaching her from the Indian burial ground: the breeze in the foliage of the pines and the branches of the birches; the flags of parchment bark flapping on the thin trunks of the birches.

But sometimes the wind could sound like a human lament.

She skirted the grass, still unexpectedly green for the time of the year, and circumspectly approached the lake. The wind bounced on the ice and assaulted her face from different directions.

She reached the spur from which, beside the alder tree, she had first noticed the opaque patch in the ice fifteen feet or so below.

The ice was thickening but still hosting air bubbles. Hands on hips, she stared defiantly across the ice on which leaves and twigs blown from the forest rested, then slithered down the bank of the spur to the rotting wooden jetty where, beneath the ice, the water was deep. The ice made noises like the rasp of a man's hand on unshaven jowls.

She peered into its grey density. Then put one mittened hand to her mouth but didn't scream – because the face peering at her was a rat's, chip-toothed and fish-eyed.

The telephone was ringing as she approached the house, just as it had been when she got back from New York city. She made a measured entrance, taking the call in the kitchen.

Mike Kaplan. Sit down, he said, be prepared for a shock. Just lately, she said, she was prepared for nothing else. She sat at the table, list of tactics in front of her. Shoot, she said.

'We're changing the date of your exhibition. Bringing it forward. Or is it backward? Anyway we're putting it on immediately after Christmas instead of January.'

'Why?'

'Because of the interest.'

'Don't give me shit, Mike. You've got a bigger name for the New Year?'

'Because you're hot, hot, hot! I've spread the word around about your nudes. Guns, knives, riding crops . . . They can't wait.'

'They?'

'The media. Immediately after Christmas is a dull time for them. They're *hunting* for stories.'

'What have you told them, Mike?'

'About the peeper. The slasher. The butterflies. Had to make a deal with them: if you want an invite, don't break the story before Christmas.'

'And you think they'll go along with that? Don't be naive, Mike. No journalist worth his salt would take any notice of an embargo like that. "Who's this guy to tell us when we can publish a story?" That's what they'll say.'

'So?' She could see his feline grin on the other end of the line.

'I can expect callers?'

'Don't turn them away, honey. But don't show them too much.' A catch of worry in his voice. 'Just one. An aperitif. *Nude Slashed*, I guess.' Hesitation. 'Do the cops know who did it?'

'They think I did.'

'Terrific.'

'That's terrific?'

'The reporters would have homed in on that one anyway.'

'So what do I tell them?'

'Hedge, baby. Hint.'

'That I did it?'

'Did you?'

'Don't make me mad, Mike. Who mutilates their own paintings?'

'Maybe you didn't like it.'

'As a matter of fact I did.'

'So, leave it open . . . Let them draw their own conclusions.'

'Jesus, for a guy with a clean-cut profile you sure have a devious mind!'

'The mind of an artistic entrepreneur,' Mike Kaplan said. 'I'm going to make you rich and famous. Harry would be proud.'

'Below the belt,' Sarah said.

'The sublime mix of the commercial painting, sensual and celebral? Don't be so fucking aesthetic, Sarah. Harry would have loved it.'

'You really think so?'

'Know so. So do you. Are you painting fast and furious?'

'I'm painting,' Sarah said.

'Good girl. *Nude Observed*?'

'How about *Nude on the Rampage*?'

'I like it.' She could see his lop-sided frown. 'I think.'

The second interruption to her preparations to drive to New York was the arrival of The Women.

They presented themselves at the front door demanding to see her latest pictures. Three of them – Mary Breeden, Josephine Mowat, and a widow with grey, watch-spring hair and a smile that also served as a frown.

'In the interests of public decency,' Mary Breeden said.

'*Public* decency? My paintings are private. They're locked in my studio.'

'But they're going to be exhibited.'

'In New York. Not here.'

'With accompanying publicity – all bad for Holyfield.'

'How can my paintings possibly affect Holyfield?'
'They already have,' Josephine Mowat said and the third woman smiled.
'If they're so lewd, why do you want to see them?'
'To make our own judgement.' Josephine Mowat stared at her with dark intensity.
'You aren't ashamed of them, are you?' Mary Breeden said.
'Give me a minute,' Sarah said. 'Come in, make yourselves at home.'
While they settled themselves cautiously she went to the studio and took the nude self-portrait from the easel. How could she have painted it? It was as though she had been possessed by a malign and prurient spirit. She took it to the garage and placed it in the trunk of the BMW.
When she returned to the house the three adjudicators were sitting on the edges of their seats. Sarah beckoned them and led them across the concrete-hard lawn still pitted with Harris's excavations. Histrionically, she threw open the door of the studio. The women entered tentatively, Sarah behind them.
Mary Breeden, invested with the voluptuous body of Pauline Crossley, seemed to leap at them.
The grey-haired widow put her hand to her mouth.
'Oh, my,' she murmured.
'Disgusting,' said Josephine Mowat.
Mary Breeden said nothing.
Their eyes swivelled to *Nude Slashed* and *Nude with a Gun*. Finally Mary Breeden spoke. 'I think we've seen enough.'
Sam Parker appeared magically at the doorway. 'Then I'll go ahead, ladies.'
'Please do,' Mary Breeden said.
The widow smiled.

Sarah called Mike half an hour later. 'You wanted a story – you've got one. I've been busted.'
'I warned you about driving that BMW too hard.'
'For obscenity. My paintings . . .'
'Jesus H. Christ!' Then: 'Okay, don't move, I'll make some calls to the media.'

'I'm driving into New York –'

'Forget it. Everyone gets lucky once in a lifetime: the trick is knowing how to adapt.'

'But –'

'Don't you hear me? Stay there on the end of your paint brush.'

Okay, so she would confront Athena tomorrow.

The media started arriving within two hours and it was soon clear that they wouldn't be content with only *Nude Slashed*.

First on the scene was Tom Kane, editor of the *Holyfield Banner* who was also local correspondent for a couple of New York newspapers and the Associated Press. He was scantily built, stooped with repressed indignation and had stayed the same age, sixtyish, ever since Sarah and Harry had moved to Holyfield. Climbing from his sagging station wagon, he held out his hand. 'Mrs Logan, I want to be the first to congratulate you. The brush is mightier than the sword.'

'You haven't seen the paintings yet.'

'I don't have to. Fact of the matter is you've created more outrage than I have in thirty years.'

'Why haven't you created it, Mr Kane? I often wondered.'

'Because I was a child of rectitude. Conceived in the dark. Born as an obligation to Mankind. Reared on conformism. By the time I came of age, Mrs Logan, the lead had been taken from my pencil.'

'Puritanism has bred many rebels, Mr Kane.'

'Depends on the genes, Mrs Logan. If your parents are creatures of compliance then the chances are you will be too.'

'Wouldn't you like to break out just once?'

Kane tapped the side of his bony nose. 'Maybe this is the time.'

'You approve of obscenity?'

'Alleged obscenity, Mrs Logan. Don't condemn yourself. Obscenity is in the eye of the beholder.'

'You must judge for yourself.' Sarah opened the door of the studio.

'Holy shit,' Kane said.

'Obscene?'

'Salutary.' He peered closer. 'That one,' pointing at *Nude Slashed*, 'says it all.'

'What does it say?'

'It indicts false morality. Pillories both the censor and the pornographer because one feeds off the other.'

'Do you find it erotic?'

'There's not much wrong with eroticism. Without it none of us would be here. Even if it does take place in the dark,' Kane said, a smile stretching the tautness of his face.

'So what are we going to do about it?'

'We?'

'You're the writer.'

'I can't pre-judge a court hearing.'

'You said the lead had been taken from your pencil. Has the film been taken from your camera?'

His hands went to the battered Pentax hanging from his neck. 'I guess not.' He removed the lens hood and aimed it at *Nude Slashed*. 'Fully exposed on the front page.' His laugh reminded Sarah of water suddenly released through rusty pipes.

The TV interviewer, who wasn't too handsome to lose credibility – a permanent frown lodged in the fleshy wedge above his nose – said: 'I'm not going to ask any questions to which you can answer a straight yes or no. One of the unwritten laws . . .'

'So what are you going to ask?' Sarah asked.

'See, you're learning already. Okay, why would a woman want to paint nudes?'

'Why not?'

'*Say* that, right? And whether *you* think they're obscene. And what your views are on accusations that you're encouraging immorality.'

'Accusations from people in the town?'

'Right. We've interviewed a lady named Mary Breeden.' He consulted his notes on a clipboard. 'And whether you think you're endangering the lives of your models. We've talked to a woman called Janice Gotthardt,' he whispered, 'and, would you believe, her dumb-shit husband is charging fifty bucks an interview?'

'You're paying?'

'It won't break us, I guess.'

'Okay. Then I'm charging a hundred dollars.'

'I like it,' the interviewer said, feeling the frown between thumb and forefinger. He raised his hand. 'Right, let's go.'

He waited a few moments. Then: 'Mrs Sarah Logan of Holyfield in upstate New York, a painter who specializes in nudes, has today been charged with offences that amount to a comprehensive indictment of obscenity. Can you first of all explain, Mrs Logan,' turning to her, 'why you, a woman, should want to paint nude women?'

'Can you think of anyone better qualified than a woman?'

'But in the public eye the painting of nudes is the prerogative of the male artist.'

'That's the way the public likes to think of it. You know, the idea has undertones of voyeurism.'

The interview proceeded along its predetermined course until: 'Sarah Logan, one last question. Why haven't you ever considered painting male nudes?'

'Because I don't like painting dicks.'

'Cut!'

The interviewer pinched his frown. 'It doesn't matter too much, because we can edit the tape. But tell me, Mrs Logan, why did you say that? I'd really like to know.'

'I guess the devil got into me.'

'Then exorcise him,' the interviewer said.

Caffrey had arrived five minutes early that morning to take Robbie to school. When they left the penthouse Caffrey's heavy head was tilted to one side as he absorbed instructions about computer infiltration.

Rebecca spent most of the day working on long-term predictions. At 4.30 p.m. she began to listen for the surge and arrival clank of the elevator. By 4.35 she was pacing the room beneath the painted stars – which was ridiculous because the time of Robbie's return depended on traffic and, in any case, at this time of the year the school timetable tended to be erratic.

At 4.40 she called the receptionist in case the elevator had broken down – not an unknown occurrence. No, it was working just fine and, no, he hadn't seen Robbie or his guardian.

At 4.45 Rebecca called the school. Mrs Skipton, theatrically exasperated, said Robbie's new minder had picked him up right outside the school – she had watched them leave together – so there was nothing to worry about, was there?

'I guess not.' Relief spread through her. 'I hope you don't mind a private detective picking up Robbie. Not so good for the school's image, I guess.'

'It's okay,' Mrs Skipton said. 'Better than a uniformed cop.'

'But he so obviously is a cop.'

'Really? He didn't strike me that way.'

'Well, he's built like one. Big and square . . .'

'He wasn't big at all,' Mrs Skipton said. 'In fact, I thought he looked more like a poet than a cop.'

Chapter Sixteen

The dreams were as bad as they had ever been, indistinguishable from reality.

She was a Nancy Fried sculpture with one breast; she was driving the BMW too fast at a child, wheel spinning ineffectually in her hands; shooting off the heads of nudes with the Mauser, hearing the cries of their owners, Harry, Ben, Mike Kaplan, Vic Gotthardt, as they were dispatched.

Ambrose pulled off his long fingers one by one; Indians opened up their graves, beckoning and pointing towards the frozen lake . . .

It was Christmas Day and the ice was cracking beneath her feet.

She cried out for help but her mouth filled with water and she awoke choking, limbs jerking as the alarm clock drilled into the dream. If that was what it was, a dream . . . She lay still, lungs weighted with water.

When the water receded she switched on the bedside lamp and looked at the clock. 5 a.m. Why had she set it so early? As her mind focused she remembered: an early morning TV call in New York!

She rolled out of bed and made her way to the bathroom, laboriously as though she were wading through the shallows of the lake. Under the shower she drowned again as water splashed into her mouth. The shower sucked in the plastic curtain, printed with blood-red poppies, and she saw the tip of an Indian scalping knife tracing the outline of her body on the other side. She swept aside the curtain, dodging as the handle of a mop slid across the plastic.

She blow-dried her hair and attended to her face. The pupils of the surprised, wide-spaced eyes regarding her from the dressing-table were dilated. Shouldn't they be contracted after sleep?

She drank two cups of black coffee to sharpen reality and consulted the fax machine, but it was too early for a horoscope.

The garden was alive with nocturnal presences but quiet. Only the stars crackled frostily. Hearing them, she thought: 'I'm going crazy. *Really* crazy.' The cold found her lungs.

She drove at a steady pace into New York, arriving at the TV studios promptly at 7.39. In make-up they tidied her hair, wiped her face, pancaked her cheeks and led her in front of the cameras and the lights. The lights illuminated the inside of her skull and she closed her eyes to keep out their questing glare.

'You okay, honey?' The interviewer was a composed blonde who could evince professional interest in anything from abominable snowmen to squirrels in Central Park.

Sarah opened her eyes. 'I'm okay.' Behind the blonde she could see a blow-up of *Nude with a Gun*.

'Right.' The blonde gesticulated at someone behind the glare. 'Now I've got to tell you, we nearly didn't make it. You know, nudes slashed at breakfast time . . . There was a lot of opposition. But we convinced them. How can we countenance censorship in this liberated age? That sort of thing. And we did point out that it wouldn't do the ratings any harm!'

Sarah's tongue was thick in her mouth. 'You like the paintings?'

'They're really something.'

The interviewer had crossed her legs and one of them swung. Sarah hoped Ambrose Moon would be watching.

'You'll make the point that we, women that is, have nothing to be ashamed about?' Sarah said. 'The fact that we can be sensual and sexual, violent even, without having to apologize?'

'Hey, who's interviewing who?' She frowned. 'Are you sure you're okay? You know, this could be one helluva an interview.'

'It will be,' Sarah said.

'Okay, we're just about to roll. Just one thing – no dicks, okay?'

'No dicks,' Sarah said as the lights again illuminated the inside of her skull.

'It's over honey,' the blonde said. 'You can come down from wherever you were.'

Sarah blinked, switching off the light in her skull. 'How was it?'

'You were one of the best.' Sarah glanced at her giveaway leg but it wasn't swinging. 'Articulate, provocative – and very sexy. But somehow I got the impression that you were talking to someone else.'

Maybe. Mary Breeden?

She would have to see Ben Deacon before she finally stepped into the abyss. But first, Rebecca Cotton.

She left the BMW in the studio parking lot and caught a cab, slumping back on the seat. She could hear the quick beat of her heart; the void left by the studio lights was ice-cold, bleak, unfathomable.

She paid off the driver at a red light and strode purposelessly down Madison. And began to feel better: a positive surge like an electric charge. A cab stopped in front of her, disgorging a sleekly prosperous man in a camel coat. She climbed in and gave the driver Rebecca Cotton's address.

A Puerto Rican girl with shiny black hair said: 'I'm sorry, Mrs Cotton doesn't see clients after the first interview.'

'Tell her it's very important.'

'It always is,' the girl said. 'But Mrs Cotton doesn't want personalities to affect her predictions.'

'How could they affect the movements of the planets?'

'The interpretations . . . The planets, nothing can change them but, you know, Mrs Cotton, she –'

'Is only human,' said Rebecca Cotton, fair-haired and chic, as Sarah remembered her, but troubled.

'Can I talk to you?' Sarah said. 'It won't take long.'

'Carmen's right. I don't encourage personal contact with clients.'

'This is terribly important.'

'Sarah Logan, isn't it?'

'You sound as though you were expecting me.'

'We *are* both Gemini, the Twins. I can spare you five minutes.' She left the connecting door open and they sat opposite each other beneath the painted stars.

'I think someone is trying to kill me,' Sarah said.

'So why come to me?'

'Because the horoscopes you fax me have forecast everything that has happened.'

'I can't emphasize too strongly that a horoscope doesn't predetermine destiny. Your will is your own.'

Sarah noticed that her eyes were smudged, pupils dilated – *like mine at 5.20 a.m.* – that the messages conveyed by her tongue seemed different to those transmitted by her fluttering fingers.

'*As darkness falls be prepared for a glimpse into the dark side of life.* That was the day I found that one of my paintings, a nude, had been slashed.'

'Your horoscope accurately predicted a sighting of malign forces. It didn't influence you . . . Shouldn't have done.'

'*An ambitious day which will culminate with unexpected freedom* . . . The day the butterflies escaped.'

'Butterflies, Sarah?'

Sarah told her about the hot-house.

'Maybe you did allow yourself to be influenced. Did *you* leave the door open?'

'It's a possibility . . .'

'You see, all astrologers do is indicate what *could* happen. In a way we are a safety valve. Don't let the stars take over . . .'

The Puerto Rican girl came in. 'You told me to remind you to call your husband.'

'Okay, Carmen. Two minutes.'

'So you're telling me that everything that has happened to me in the past few weeks was written in the stars, but I could have taken evasive action?'

"'The fault, dear Brutus, is not in our stars, but in ourselves.'"

'You're telling me the absolute truth?'

'Of course. If I didn't believe I wouldn't practise. Gaze up at the stars on a deep clear night: they talk to you.'

She shook her hand, palm facing Sarah.

'What shall I do Mrs Cotton? I'm scared.'

'Look into the sky, Sarah.' Again she moved her hand.

'Can you give me today's prediction?'

'It's been transmitted.'

The Puerto Rican girl said: 'Your husband is on the line, Mrs Cotton.'

'But surely –'

'After we've transmitted horoscopes, we destroy them. It will be waiting for you when you get home. Now if you will excuse me . . . Hallo, Will,' she said, hand tight on the phone.

Sarah called Ben Deacon but his receptionist said he wouldn't be there till later so she caught another cab to SoHo and wandered round the galleries planning to lunch at Da Silvano. A.I.R. on Crosby Street, Mary Boone, Castelli and Ivan Karp's O.K. Harris Works of Art on West Broadway, SoHo 20 on Broome Street . . . At an exhibition of Daisy Youngblood's wood and clay sculptures – mostly incomplete female torsos hunched with pain, animals with blind, reproachful eyes – her mind began to echo. The single wooden arm on a torso with a gently swelling belly reached for her, eyes moved in the empty sockets of a gorilla's head.

She stumbled into the street. Leaned against a wall. Deep-breathed sanity. Finding a phone booth, she called Ben Deacon's number again. He had returned but he was with a patient and couldn't be disturbed. 'No, not even for you, Mrs Logan.' But there was a cancellation at 11.30.

The prospect of seeing Ben tranquillized her. She called at Mike Kaplan's gallery and found him in a state of euphoria, newspapers spread across his desk. And, yes, he had caught her on the early morning TV show, and, yes, he had taped it. Did she want to see herself?

The last thing she wanted.

'Associated Press put out a piece so almost every newspaper coast to coast had the story. You're notorious, Sarah, much more profitable than being famous. How many more can you paint before the exhibition now the date's been changed?'

'None.' She remembered with a shock that *Nude Observed* was still in the trunk of the BMW.

'None?' He looked as though he had been slapped.

'I don't feel like painting any more. I haven't been feeling so good recently.'

'You've got to be kidding. This is the once-in-a-lifetime . . .'

She relented. 'Okay, maybe a couple more. Then . . .'

'What, for Christ's sake?'

'I don't know. I'm not a good painter, Mike.'

'You're a genius.'

'You know that's not true. The only yardstick for genius is originality and that I don't have.'

'*Nude Slashed* isn't original?'

'Only the lucky idea, not the technique. I'm derivative and that's not good enough.'

'You have to learn from other painters.'

'Sure, but not sub-consciously plagiarize, and that's what I do.'

'So what are you going to do, still lifes? Wine bottle with half eaten pomegranate?'

'I'm not sure I'm going to paint anything.'

'So what are you going to do?'

'Dance,' Sarah said. 'Write. Take photographs . . . I don't know. Thanks to Harry I don't have any money problems, never will. Maybe I'll take up astrology!'

Mike Kaplan clearly didn't believe her. 'Okay, we'll talk about it after Christmas. But don't let me down – three more pictures.'

'Two.'

'Two and a half.'

From the gallery she caught the fourth cab of the morning – and it was still only eleven – to Deacon's consulting rooms. Watched by the disapproving receptionist, a gingery woman in starched white, he escorted her into his living-room and placed her in an easy chair from which she could pick up the cramped glint of the East River.

She told him about the hallucinations.

'Not as uncommon as you might think. Stress can bring them on.'

'Hearing *colours*?'

'Sure, why not? All our senses are correlated. That old trick of getting someone to identify different drinks with their eyes closed – they usually get it wrong. In any case we're only dealing with descriptions invented by inadequate Man. The taste of strawberries *is* pink; the smell of steak frying *is* brown.'

'So I'm not going crazy?'

'If you're crazy, the Pope's a Protestant.' He grinned, a dove instead of a hawk. 'You're not on a trip, are you? Acid, Ecstasy . . .'

'Toasted pitta for breakfast.'

'I can give you a sedative.'

'No,' she said. 'That's just sweeping everything under the carpet. I've got to fight.'

'We've got to fight,' he said. 'I've made some progress. That licence plate on the green car . . . The cops have been helpful in an unenthusiastic sort of way but, of course, the numbers and letters were jumbled. Anyway they've come up with ten possible owners and I'm checking them out.'

'Regular little Dick Tracy.'

'And you're a regular little smart-ass celebrity. I saw you on TV this morning.'

'How was I?'

'Okay. No, really. But somehow it wasn't you.'

'It wasn't,' Sarah said.

'You really don't want a sedative?'

'I've got this stuff to make me sleep. That's just fine for now.'

'Yeah, well . . .' He paced the room. 'Is there anything else?'

She told him about the phone call to her house from the studio outside and the fake Mauser that had suddenly become real.

'Okay, we can check out the gun. Have you checked out your star-gazer?'

'A couple of hours ago – she couldn't help.'

'How could she? Heavenly bodies don't substitute loaded guns for fakes.'

'She believes,' Sarah said. 'She really does.'

'And you?'

'You can't discount the stars.'

'Not assertive enough. You either believe or you don't.'

'Bullshit.' Resentment between therapist and reluctant patient surfaced. 'What's wrong with being a don't-know? I never understood why Doubting Thomas was supposed to be such a creep.'

'What am I supposed to say: "I like you when you're angry"?'

'Your problem is that because you delve into pyschosomatics you consider yourself to be a superior mortal. What you can't understand is spontaneity, irrational behaviour.'

'Wrong. I deal in irrational behaviour.'

'Wrong. You deal in what you've been *taught* is irrational.'

He stood up abruptly. 'See what I mean? No therapist should ever get involved with a patient.'

'Christ,' she said. 'And you called me a smart-ass.'

He walked to the window and stared at the glimpse of river. 'I want a list of everyone who hates you.'

'If I have enough paper. Every pillar of respectability in Holyfield, to start with.'

'Why won't you stay here?'

'Ginger Rogers wouldn't approve.'

'Ginger Rogers?'

'Your receptionist,' Sarah said.

He took her for lunch at The Four Seasons. She apologized over the Chocolate Velvet.

At 2.30 she picked up the BMW from the studio parking lot and headed for home.

The little girl, hair in bunches, stared out of the dusk, an under-exposed snapshot taken with an antique camera.

Sarah trod on the brake pedal. Nothing. The BMW continued inexorably towards the child on the approach road to Holyfield.

Mouth frozen open, hands palming away pain . . .

Sarah swung the wheel. The BMW slewed to the right and went into a skid on the black ice. Sarah saw the girl's face slide to her left. Now the rear of the car would strike her.

She swung the wheel the opposite way. Felt the BMW waltz. A bump. On the rear fender? Ahead a brick wall, branches of a willow tree weeping over it . . .

The impact was brutal; she felt it in the joints of her bones. Glass broke, metal groaned. She switched off the engine, laid her head on the wheel.

The door opened and a face, Josephine Mowat's, peered in.

'Are you okay?'

'The girl . . .'

'She's fine.'

'I felt a bump.'

'You hit her teddy bear,' Josephine Mowat said. 'You didn't do that a whole lot of good.'

Dr Storr put away his instruments in his bag. 'You'll live,' he said. 'Superficial cuts and contusions, nothing more.'

She saw him to the door, then hurried to the fax machine to read her prediction for the day that was moving swiftly to its conclusion: only five hours of it left.

Chapter Seventeen

You must obey the planets to allay the dark forces of the mind so that you can find lasting peace . . .

After Sarah Logan had left, Carmen Barea entered the room. 'You should have given her the horoscope,' she said.
 'How much are they paying you, Carmen?' There was a tightness in Rebecca's chest and she tried to breathe it away.
 'Enough to get me out of the pits they call a home.'
 'You should have told me. I could have helped.'
 'You *knew*. You did nothing.'
 'Were you working with them right from the start?'
 Carmen shook her head and her polished hair danced. 'No, they – the guy with the sad face, that is – approached me in the street a week or so before he came busting in here.'
 'Who are they, Carmen?'
 'Sure as hell don't know, Mrs Cotton. All I know is, I've to make sure you send the right horoscopes to Sarah Logan and don't do anything stupid.'
 'Would I do anything stupid? They've got my son, they've got Robbie . . .'
 She reached out and touched the telephone that had rung immediately she had cut off Mrs Skipton.

'Mrs Cotton?' It had been the voice of the man with the poet's face.
 'Where's Robbie? What's happened to him?' Wings of fear beat inside her.
 'Robbie's fine, and he won't come to any harm if you do what you're told. You have my word on it.'

'Where is he? Where's my son?'

'He's okay is all you need to know. Now listen.' A cutting edge to his voice. 'Don't call the cops, don't call your husband, no one. You got it?'

'I understand.'

'All you got to do is send the Logan woman certain horoscopes.' He pronounced it "horrorscopes". 'Carmen Barea will tell you what they are.'

'*Carmen?*'

'Sure. She's with us.'

Rebecca held the receiver away from her as though it were contaminated. *Carmen?*

'Are you still there, Mrs Cotton?'

'Why can't *she* send them? I promise I won't interfere if you release Robbie.'

'Because she hasn't got the know-how. Your clients wouldn't believe her; most of all Sarah Logan wouldn't believe her. Leave Carmen in charge and Athena would be in deep shit. No, it's got to be you, Mrs Cotton.'

'What sort of horoscopes?'

'First tell her she's got to obey the planets.'

'She wouldn't believe that. All my clients are told they have a will of their own.'

'Not Sarah Logan.'

'What do you mean, not Sarah Logan?'

A smoker's phlegmy cough. 'She's been conditioned. She'll do what she's told.'

'Conditioned?'

'You don't realize how much you've helped us. You and Carmen Barea.'

'I don't understand,' Rebecca said. Her bottom lip began to tremble.

'No reason why you should. But when it's all over – and you have my word on it, Robbie will come home to Mama safe and sound – you'll understand everything. If you don't cooperate . . . Poor Caffrey.'

'What happened to Caffrey?'

'He's indisposed. You wouldn't want Robbie to be indisposed, would you, Mrs Cotton?'

'If you let him go free, I'll –' but halfway through the sentence she realized she was addressing a dead line.

She sat for a few moments with her hands to her face, eyes closed, bars of red light striating the darkness. Then she remembered: *whatever predictions I send Sarah Logan are mine as well. Gemini. Twins.*

'I *should* tell them, Mrs Cotton,' Carmen Barea said.
  'Tell them what?'
  'That you didn't give Mrs Logan her horoscope.'
  'Why. for God's sake?'
  'They want to know everything.'
  'Does it matter? She'll read it when she gets home.'
  'Too late, I think.' Carmen Barea fished a St Christopher pendant from the foothills of her firm young breasts and bit it with her sharp teeth. 'Why did you lie to her about destroying the horoscopes?'
  'Because part of the prediction was true: I felt it. It was something she had to deal with. Interfere with the prophecies of the planets and you're interfering with destiny.'
  'I know what you mean, I guess. Believe me, Mrs Cotton, I'm sorry –'
  'That my son's life is in danger? Don't give me shit, Señorita Barea.'
  'I've always admired you.'
  'You didn't hear me, did you?'
  The phone rang. Carmen Barea picked it up and handed over the receiver. 'For you. Your son.'
  'Hi, Mom.'
  'Robbie, are you okay?'
  'I'm okay but I want to come home.' A catch in his voice.
  'Soon,' Rebecca said.
  'When's soon? I don't understand. This man, your friend, says you're sick.'
  'I didn't feel so hot but I'm getting better.'
  'Can't I stay with Dad?'
  'We'll see,' Rebecca said.
  'Because of the witch?'
  'Don't call her that.'
  '*You* do,' Robbie said. 'I just don't –' A sob in his voice.
  'You're getting on all right with . . . my friend?'
  'Sure, he's a nice guy. Lets me play on his computer.'

'Have you got through to the Pentagon yet?'

'I'm working on it,' Robbie said. 'Mom –'

But what ever he wanted to say to Mom she never knew because the receiver was suddenly inanimate in her hand. She replaced it.

'I'm sure he'll be okay, Mrs Cotton,' Carmen Barea said. 'And I won't tell them you lied to Mrs Logan.'

'Oh, sure, he'll be okay. But will you? Why don't you consult *your* stars, Carmen?'

She kicked shut the connecting door, slumped, and, for the first time since the call to Mrs Skipton, wept.

Chapter Eighteen

You must obey the planets . . .

Sarah, trying to relax with a Martini after the accident, had never read such a horoscope: a command, not a forecast. She poured more Martini from the shaker into her glass.

Beware of peril on the roads.

She called the garage in Holyfield and told the mechanic to check whether the brakes on the BMW had been tampered with.

Why hadn't Rebecca given her the prediction in her office? In retrospect Sarah didn't believe that she destroyed all the horoscopes. She called Rebecca Cotton's number, but only got through to the answering machine.

Tonight you will make a trip to atone for the past. To a deserted place where you once shared the future.

It had to be the old clap-board house where she and Harry had sheltered one rainy afternoon when they were house-hunting: wind blustering the rain against the grimy windows, sighing in the rafters, a door banging . . . He had fetched a travelling rug from the car and they had made love on the floor.

'Will we always be together?' she had asked.

'Always. Even after death.'

It will occur to you that you can join the person with whom you shared.

Technical details about the positions of the planets followed.

Some horoscope! Anyone who took such a prediction seriously was crazy. She switched on the TV with the remote control: One of those family sitcoms in which everyone was always eating breakfast. A newscast – a traffic pile-up on Palisades Interstate Parkway, icy conditions blamed . . .

It couldn't do any harm to walk to the old house, could it? That wasn't being manipulated – more an act of defiance.

Don't do it, Sarah.

She finished the Martini, put on the moulting beaver jacket and jeans, fetched a flashlight and let herself out.

The deserted house stood on the other side of town close to the sawmill and she walked at a resolute pace. Frozen mud crunched beneath her boots, stars peered from rents in the clouds. Muffled voices reached her from the direction of the Indian burial ground but the forest always talked at night.

In the town she met Ambrose Moon emerging from Noveck's.

'Don't like the hunch of those shoulders, Mrs Logan.'

'Just the cold.' She straightened up.

'You should stand up to the cold, Mrs Logan. Make an ally of it.' He took his hands from the pockets of his topcoat and rubbed his long fingers together.

'What would you say if I made this gesture to you?' Sarah took off a mitten and shook her hand, palm facing him.

'Right now? Nothing. Gestures all relate to circumstances.'

'The person who made the gesture was trying to reassure me. About astrology, in fact.'

'Trying to reassure you?' Ambrose Moon pulled one finger, clicking a joint. 'Well, maybe he was –'

'She.'

'– but she was also trying to warn you.'

'About what?'

'That I wouldn't know, Mrs Logan. Was there anyone else present?'

'A Puerto Rican girl.'

'Then I figure she was trying to warn you without that girl knowing. Now you're beginning to hunch over again, Mrs Logan. If I can be of any help, you know where to find me. Milkshakes on me.'

Straightening up again, Sarah made her way along the deserted street, past cosily lit houses, towards the sawmill half a mile away. Fifty yards past the last house she turned on to the path beside the road and switched on the flashlight. Clouds closed over the stars and darkness pushed at its beam, a cat, or a fox, crossed her path.

A car pulled up and a man with a mottled face wound down the window. 'This is no night for walking, lady. Get in and I'll take you to wherever you want.'

'Thank you,' she said, 'but I'm okay. Really.'

He opened the door. 'Come on, honey, it's warm in here.'

'I told you –'

'And cosy, real cosy.'

She slammed the door, shone the beam of the flashlight in his face.

'I've got your licence number. Now get lost, mister, or I'll report you to the cops for harassment.'

'Sorry lady.' He held up his hands. 'Just trying to be a Good Samaritan.' As he took off he shouted: 'Don't worry – you'll get yours.'

She walked on, beam of the flashlight a mine detector. A light burned in the mill; she could hear the rip of saw against wood, smell sawdust and resin. The old house lay to the right, a couple of hundred yards from the mill. To reach it she had to walk down an overgrown lane and brambles and branches reached for her in the darkness.

The door opened with a creak. The flashlight found cobwebs, a hanging rafter, a mattress, the red eyes of a rodent. Wings beat the air and a bird flew out of a broken window.

She followed the beam up the wooden stairs. A step snapped and she fell against the wooden rail: a groan of rotten wood and the rail swung away. She flung herself back and leaned, sobbing, against the wall.

Five more steps and she was on the landing. The door of the room where they had made love was open.

The beam explored the floorboards. The travelling rug, she remembered, had been tartan.

She smelled cigar smoke.

Downstairs a door banged.

She began to descend the stairs, steps snapping like decayed teeth. She heard the voice when she was half way down. Male, outside the house, indistinct. 'Always . . . even . . . death.'

She took another step forward – into the space left by the step that had broken on her way up. She fell heavily and slid on her back down the remaining steps. The flashlight dropped from her hand and the light went out.

The darkness was palpable. Tripping, stumbling, she reached the door. It was shut. Obdurate.

She listened to the beat of her heart, to the scutter of rodents. To the voice: 'Must join me in death.' *His voice*?

She leaned into the mould-smelling darkness, arms outstretched, feeling her way towards the rear of the house. A floorboard broke and her leg plunged through the invisible gap. She heard her jeans tear, felt blood warm on her calf. She blundered on towards a rectangle of dark marginally lighter than the blackness crowding her. A door. Open.

She fell, heard glass break. She got to her feet and made a blind run towards the escape hatch.

Then she was outside and the night air was fresh on her cheeks and ahead of her was a vista, an avenue perhaps – she couldn't remember – leading to the lighted sawmill.

She ran towards it. Her bruised chest ached as she gulped cold air.

The bright cavern of the mill grew nearer. She could see a circular saw slicing the trunk of a tree. The teeth of the saw shone brightly and she was racing towards them and she could feel them ripping her chest.

She ran faster, thighs pistons, feeling the heat generated by the saw.

Screamed as arms grabbed her from behind the doors of the mill, pinioning her.

'Hey, now where the hell do you think you're going?' Vic Gotthardt said.

Janice Gotthardt poured red wine. 'Vic says you were really steaming. What were you doing in that place anyway?'

'Harry and I used to go there.'

'At night?'

'In the summer. When we were looking for somewhere to live.'

'I can imagine,' Vic Gotthardt said.

'I'll bet you can,' his wife said.

Sarah took in the room. Tacky – walls spattered with the detritus of domestic strife – but comfortable in a discarded sort of way. She drank the wine; it was rough, but it lined her stomach with velvet.

'What were you running away from?' Vic Gotthardt asked.

'From the devil.'

'Don't put me on.'

'I dropped my flashlight. It was dark. I got scared.'

'You nearly sliced yourself in half on the saw.'

'I've been getting a lot of calls since the publicity,' Janice said. 'A lot of painters want me to model for them. An agency too.'

'Terrific.'

'But I'd rather model for you.'

'I'd like that too,' Vic Gotthardt said.

'Why, for God's sake? You'd make much more money with an agency.'

'Money isn't everything,' he said with dignity.

Janice filled her mouth with wine, explored it with her tongue, swallowed. 'If you really want to know,' she said thickly, 'Vic likes to keep it local.'

'With me?'

'If you really want to know,' Janice said, winking elaborately, 'Vic would like to watch.'

Remembering the face in the sky-light, Sarah asked if she might call a cab.

The headlamps of the cab lit up the licence plate of Gotthardt's green Dodge. But the number bore no relation to the garbled one she had remembered during hypermnesia.

If, that was, she had remembered accurately, she thinks as she begins to drift into sleep. But surely she must have, because the digits and the E had related plausibly to ten possible owners.

She closes her eyes. Ben's voice. 'You see it in the driving mirror. In a frame. It registers in your mind. What make of car?'

'A Dodge, maybe. Chev, Toyota . . . only caught a glimpse.'

But she remembers the driver. Remembers that he had the face of a poet.

Chapter Nineteen

Make preparations to step into the future that awaits us all. Only two days to Christmas . . .

Harry had proposed on Christmas Day.

There were two other faxes and she took them into the kitchen. One from Ben. *Tried to call you last night but you must have been out cold. Have narrowed down the owner of the green car to three. Following up other line of enquiry too. Could be on to something. Call me after your first yawn because I have to visit a patient at 9 a.m. Luv, Ben.*

She glanced at the wall clock. 9.10.

The second fax was from Mike Kaplan. *So where were you? I tried both lines last night, zilch. Be prepared for a lunch visitor – nothing fattening. I want to pick up the paintings you've finished so far. That's it, back to your easel.*

She went outside to collect the mail – Christmas cards, mostly – and the *Holyfield Banner*. No nudes on the front page, only seasonal greetings and a black and white photograph of a snow-covered Holyfield fifty years earlier. Tom Kane, you wimp! *Nude Slashed* was on the centre-fold, accompanied by an editorial explaining why it was in the public interest to publish it – the pending court case affected 'the moral rationale' of Holyfield and readers of the *Banner* were entitled to decide whether it was obscene or whether it was an indictment of false morality.

The phone rang. Kane's nasal voice. 'Seen the *Banner*, Mrs Logan?'

'*Playboy* and *Penthouse* had better look to their guns.'

'Sorry I couldn't put her on the front page – she isn't exactly festive.'

'And she'd freeze to death.'

'The reason I'm calling is to thank you.'

'For what, Mr Kane?'

'You've put the lead back in my pencil.'

The call pleased her more than anything that had happened for a long time. The night's dreams receded, and the day asserted itself. She made coffee and opened the cards, placing them on the mantel above the fireplace in the living-room. The cards were from her parents – A FLORIDA CHRISTMAS TREE, i.e. an orange tree – a couple of students, now married with children, from Pratt, the owner of a new gallery in the TriBeCa area of New York city . . .

The penultimate card, robins and traditional glitter, looked vaguely familiar. Frowning, she opened it and read the scrawl beneath the printed greeting. *From Harry, forever.*

The day reeled again. Her voice echoed in her ears; the splash of water from the shower was silver.

The card was one of a dozen they had bought in Macy's. She had seen it lying on top of a chest of drawers in the spare room only the other day. She opened the door; it was gone, of course – only a polished rectangle in the dust testifying to its existence.

Could she have sent it? Simulated Harry's handwriting? Had she taken the knife from the drawer in the kitchen and slashed the painting of Janice Gotthardt? Imagined the voice outside the deserted house? Was she quite mad?

The phone summoned her to the kitchen; it was Ben Deacon. 'Are you okay?'

She said she was fine. How could she tell him that she had heard Harry's voice, sent herself a Christmas card?

'You sound a long way off.'

She moved the receiver closer to her mouth. 'I'm right here.'

'That's better. There's a lot I want to tell you.' Suppressed excitement in his voice. 'But I can't, not yet. Soon. Why don't you stay with me over Christmas?'

Because you don't want a crazy woman staying with you. 'Thanks, Ben, but I've got to stick it out here.'

'How about inviting me up there?'

'Christmas Eve? Okay. What sort of diamonds are you buying me?'

'Only paste,' he said. 'But I worry about you up there. Take good care now. Lock yourself in at night.'

'Ben, why would anyone want to follow me in a car?'

'To get evidence?'

'Of what?'

A pause. 'That you were acting . . . strangely?' Another pause. 'Were you?'

'I pointed the fake gun at my head and said "Bang".'

'There you go, that sort of thing.'

'I was just kidding.'

'Might sound kind of weird in the telling.'

'Sorry I'm not a model of rectitude.'

'I suppose you read your horoscope this morning?'

Oh, yes, she said, she had read that all right.

'Because I removed the post-hypnotic suggestion.'

'I would have read it anyway.'

'Maybe. Because you didn't want the suggestion in the first place – which is why you're becoming hostile now.'

'Maybe Christmas Eve isn't such a good idea,' Sarah said, and replaced the red telephone on the wall bracket.

Pale flakes drifted past the studio window. Was it snowing? She opened the door and stepped out.

There was a faint smell of burning, the wail of a siren. She cupped her hand and caught a flake. Ash.

She ran into town.

The firemen were directing looping jets of water on to the offices of the *Holyfield Banner* which were burning energetically. A crowd stood on the perimeter of the roped-off area. She spotted Ambrose Moon, Mary Breeden, Vic Gotthardt, and some of the loiterers from the inner sanctum of the library.

She summoned Sam Parker who, uniformed, was patrolling the area beyond the ropes with swaggering authority. 'Hey!'

Parker approached. 'Was there something, Mrs Logan?'

'How did this start?'

'Maybe you should ask yourself that.'

'How did it start, for Christ's sake?'

'*Nude Slashed*. Lot of people round these parts don't like that sort of thing.'

'Arson?'

'Whatever you say, Mrs Logan.'

'Do you have any leads?'

'Only the artist who caused the provocation in the first place.'

'Fuck you, Officer Parker. Maybe I should do another painting. *Cop's Cock Subsiding*.'

'See you in court, Mrs Logan.'

A breeze fanned the burning building and flames brushed the adjoining premises, the consulting rooms of Dr Storr. The jets of the hoses moved with the flames, the steam hissing from the walls. The spectators sighed. Embers rose into the sky like orange maggots.

Mary Breeden, Josephine Mowat and a couple of other women stood at the front of the crowd, arms crossed stoically.

Ambrose Moon said: 'Just you look at those postures.'

'I thought you were working on *gestures*.'

'Postures are frozen gestures.'

'You think they started the fire?'

'Can't say, Mrs Logan. But they're . . . how would you put it? Aggressively defensive.'

Charred copies of the *Banner* fluttered from the burning building, skipping beyond the heat of the flames; dismembered limbs of *Nude Slashed* settled on the street. A roar went up from the crowd as the roof of the building collapsed.

Tom Kane, thin frame erect, joined Sarah. 'Some fire,' he said. 'It would have made the front page of the *Banner* – but, of course, there won't be any *Banner*.'

'I'm sorry,' Sarah said.

'No need to be. Associated Press will have the story – EDITOR ACCUSES ARSONISTS OF PLOT TO DESTROY FREE SPEECH.'

'You don't care?'

'Oh, I care all right. Can you understand what it means to me? Most of my life I've been reporting news, dodging anything controversial. Then all of a sudden, I *am* news. So is the *Banner*. Makes it all seem worthwhile.'

Another jet of water rose from a newly arrived engine and fell hissing into the fire. The flames flagged and the crowd began to disperse.

'Know what I'd do, Mrs Logan, as an old hack with a nose for news?' Tom Kane said.

'What would you do, Tom?'

'I'd get the hell back to my home and make sure nothing has happened to that studio of mine.'

Sarah looked round; but of Mary Breeden and Josephine Mowat there was no sign.

The fire was inside the studio, crackling and spitting as it devoured paint and canvas, and there was a smell of gasoline in the air. Backing away from the heat, Sarah stood beside the butterfly house and watched the studio burn.

Mike Kaplan arrived in his station wagon; jumping out, he ran towards her. 'Shit!' he shouted, punching the palm of his left hand. 'It would have been some exhibition . . . Have you called Emergency?'

'Let it burn.' She led him into the house and showed him the paintings she had taken into the living-room that morning to cover in plastic to protect them en route to New York.

He embraced her. 'You're a wonderful woman, know that?'

A small victory, Sarah thought. Her first. Her last.

Releasing her, Mike Kaplan said: 'How about *Nude Burning*?'

Chapter Twenty

Dawn tomorrow is the time . . .

Christmas Eve.
    Rebecca Cotton read the horoscope she had faxed to Sarah Logan. *Dawn tomorrow* was the time for what?
    Carmen Barea came into her office. 'There's a call for you.'
    'Who?'
    'Pick up the receiver.'
    It was Robbie. 'Hi, Mom.'
    'Hallo, darling. Are you all right?'
    'I'm okay but I don't understand . . .'
    'I know you don't, Robbie. I'll try and explain when you come home.'
    'Tomorrow's Christmas Day. Will I be home?'
    'I hope so, honey.'
    'I don't understand . . .'
    'It's for your own good.'
    'Are you really ill?'
    'I'll live.'
    'If you're not that bad, why can't I come home?'
    'Trust me.'
    'Okay.' A silence kept alive by the sound of his breathing, so quick that it reminded her of his breathing when he was born. 'I trust you.'
    'Are they looking after you all right?'
    '*They*? There's only one of them. Sure, he's a nice guy. Except that he smokes too much.'
    Another voice. 'Cm'on, Robbie.'

'Mom –'
'Robbie –'
The vibrant silence of severance. She replaced the receiver.
'There's another call for you,' Carmen Barea said. 'I've kept it on hold.'
'What's going on?' Will said.
'Nothing's going on.'
'That was a long call you were taking.'
'A client forgot the rules.'
'It's Christmas Eve.'
'So?'
'We haven't bought Robbie's presents.'
'Can you do that, Will?'
'Sure. What presents?'
'We made lists, right?'
'I thought we'd both –'
'I'm very busy. You know, extended forecasts for Christmas, New Year . . .'
'They're more important than shopping for your son?'
'Don't start, Will.'
'Okay, I'm sorry. I'll be over tomorrow – for the whole day.'
Carmen Barea was standing in front of her, shaking her head, showing her a newspaper, one item ringed with blue ink. A private detective named David Caffrey had been found in his apartment. Dead. Knifed.
'About tomorrow . . .' Rebecca said.
'What about tomorrow? I've told Beth I'm coming. She said okay. Under duress, I guess. But, shit, if you can't allocate one day of the year to your son –'
Carmen Barea was shaking her head energetically. Rebecca saw the knife being withdrawn from Caffrey's square chest, blade applied to Robbie's neck. Carmen Barea wrote on a leaf of a pad and placed it in front of Rebecca. *NEW HAMPSHIRE.*
'As a matter of fact we're going to spend Christmas with my parents.'
'What are you talking about, for Christ's sake?'
'They've taken a place near Exeter.'
'I don't believe what I'm hearing!'

'It would be nice for Robbie.'

'What the hell are you talking about? You, me, Robbie – we always spend Christmas together.'

'You were talking about sharing some of it with Beth.' She regretted the words immediately.

'You haven't been close to your parents for years.'

'Perhaps now's the time to change that.'

'Rebecca, there's something wrong, isn't there?'

'Nothing, Will, really.'

'You're lying – I've known you too long.'

'No –'

'I'm coming round now.'

'No, please . . .' Her hand inched across the desk, fingers finding the handle of a paper knife.

'Now.'

'I – we – won't be here.'

'Stay there, please, Rebecca.'

Carmen Barea was signalling frantically.

'I'm sorry –'

'Please, for Robbie's sake.'

'Merry Christmas, Will.'

'I'm on my way.'

Carmen Barea took the receiver from her, cut the call with one slender, olive-skinned finger.

Rebecca placed her own finger-tips to her eyes, pressed hard. Dismissed the planets. *Please, God. Help me.*

Chapter Twenty-One

Dawn tomorrow is the time . . .

A terrible exultancy had replaced the aberrations and Sarah acted decisively. She showered, dressed and sat down to write her last letters.

> Dear Ben,
> I want to thank you for everything but there are forces abroad in the universe that transcend all terrestrial phenomena. I know now what I have to do and I welcome the knowledge. Perhaps the outcome would have been different if you hadn't honoured the relationship between therapist and patient, but then again that was written in the heavens. As is birth – and death. Take good care, Ben, and when the right girl comes along, go easy on the honour!

She smiled, signed the letter, folded it and slipped it into an envelope.

The second note, to her parents, was more difficult. She poured coffee and stared out of the kitchen window into the garden. The cold had gone from the sky and the garden breathed once more.

She picked up the pen. They believed they had been good parents – had been by conventional standards. Was there any need to blight their autumnal years with recrimination?

She opened the envelope containing the note to Ben and added a postscript. *Please treat this as a private farewell – no one else need know that it isn't an accident.*

She heard her mother's voice. 'It was God's will,' and her father, 'We gave her a good home and she had a good life.'

Mike Kaplan? No need. He had the paintings; although there wouldn't be anymore, the news of her accident would dramatically increase their value.

Her attorney? Pointless again. Her will was in order: in due course the Society for Distressed Artists would be richer by more than two million dollars and many painters far better than herself would be given the opportunity to express themselves.

She went upstairs, put the note to Ben in the bedside table and dressed magnificently: navy suit, white cashmere sweater, ranch mink. On the way out she touched Harris's blanket and, outside, closed the door of the butterfly house. The studio was a pile of blackened rubble.

She strode towards Holyfield with aplomb, pausing at the lacrosse field to watch a hell-raising game between two teams of men. Noticing her in her splendour one player saluted her with his stick. She swept on, the exultancy still upon her; but from time to time shark fins of ultimate fear broke its surface.

In the main street recorded bells and the voices of a children's choir issued through loudspeakers. A tall Christmas tree hung with lights stood in front of the church. Women shopped with last-minute ferocity; a group of teenagers stood watching firemen and investigators ferret in the wreckage of the *Banner*.

Sarah called first on Mary Breeden, who was sitting at her desk sorting a pile of children's annuals. Pale sunshine filtered through the window lighting the crib beside the desk.

'I'm looking for some Christmas reading,' Sarah said.

'Really? What did you have in mind?' She didn't look up from the annuals.

'Whatever sort of pornography you recommend.'

The polished blonde hair seemed to tighten. 'I think we can postpone any references to obscenity for your trial.'

'No, come on. The really hot stuff you keep under the counter after you've read it.'

Mary Breeden raised her head from the annuals. 'If you don't get out of here right now, I'll call the police.'

'Nosey Parker? Ah, I get it. He wants the porn first, right?'

Mary Breeden picked up the telephone.

Sarah held up one hand. 'Don't bother. I really came in to tell you the good news.'

'Good news?'

'I got all the nudes out of the studio before you burned it down.' She smiled. 'Have yourself a steamy, steamy Christmas, Mrs Breeden.'

She met Sam Parker across the street. 'Morning, Sam.' He tried to walk round her but she blocked him. 'I called police headquarters at Albany this morning.'

'So?'

'You never sent those prints to the lab, did you?'

'Can't discuss a case when it's pending, Mrs Logan. You should know that.'

'Because you didn't really believe they matched. Much easier to keep them in your office and practise a little erotic blackmail. Well, I'll tell you something – they *would* have matched.'

'If you say so.'

'And I'll tell you something else – I've filed a complaint against you for dereliction of duty. Merry Christmas, Officer Parker.'

Taking the lie with her, she walked into Noveck's for a last milkshake with Ambrose Moon.

'Wow,' he exclaimed.

'Wow what?'

'Some change!'

She sat down and ordered a chocolate milkshake: unseasonable but just what she needed. 'Change?'

'Your shoulders, your hands . . . You're defiant, Mrs Logan, know that?' He frowned and took a swig of root beer. 'More than defiant – triumphant, in a negative way. Is that possible?' The frown deepened.

'I'm triumphant all right, Mr Moon, no question.'

'Can you elaborate?'

Loose-wristed, she waved her hand in front of him.

'Something big has come up? Not true, Mrs Logan. Don't put me on.'

She let her shoulders sag. 'Better?'

'I don't know . . . You confuse me. I've never seen so much contradiction in one person.'

'Remember me fondly, Mr Moon.'

'Don't talk like that. Talk with your hands – they're more honest than tongues.'

'They can lie.'

'Not to me.'

She lowered her hand, allowing the fingers to droop.

'You mean that?' Ambrose Moon asked.

'You know I do.'

'Call me before you do anything –'

She pointed one finger at him. *Okay* – another lie. And he read it.

'Goodbye, Mr Moon.' She stuck out her hand but he didn't take it.

'Merry Christmas, Mrs Logan.'

'You know better than that.' She placed one hand over his long, thin fingers, and squeezed gently and walked into the street where the bells and the voices of young people hung on golden caskets.

The mechanic at the garage was unable to say whether or not anyone had tampered with the brakes of the BMW. Not that she cared anymore. She took *Nude Observed* from the trunk, tucked it under her arm and strode purposefully home. There she tossed it on to the charred rubble of the studio, drenched it with gasoline, fired it with a match and watched it burn.

Ben Deacon arrived at six. 'Despite the patient-shrink hostility on the phone,' he said, handing her a small, gift-wrapped package. 'I vote we suspend hostilities over Christmas.'

She kissed him on the cheek, touched the skin beneath his eyes with the tips of her fingers.

'What was *that* all about?'

Ambrose Moon would have known, she thought.

'Can I open it?' She held up the package.

'Go ahead – it's Christmas Day somewhere in the world.'

Diamonds – a pendant. It saddened her immeasurably. 'Thank you, Ben.' She stretched out her hand, let it fall.

'Paste,' he said.

'Not this.' She held the pendant up to the light and stars sparkled.

She lit the log fire in the living-room, poured him a bourbon on the rocks, a Scotch for herself. 'I'm sorry the house isn't more festive,' she said.

'Don't worry: I'm more tired than festive. Over-tired. I couldn't sleep last night, so tonight I'll take one of your sedatives.'

'You're staying the night?'

'Try and stop me,' Ben Deacon said.

'How could I, wearing this?' She touched the pendant at her throat. 'I'll make up a bed in the spare room.'

'Last time –'

'Was last time. I've got a lot to do. Preparations for tomorrow . . . I don't want to disturb you. In any case, you'll be dead to the world.'

A log moved and sparks chased each other up the chimney.

Ben went out to his car, returning with an overnight bag and more parcels. He opened them in the kitchen. 'I went crazy. Irish smoked salmon from Connemara – a big thank you to Federal Express; a ham from Smithfield, Virginia; steam-peeled chestnuts from Alachua, Florida . . .'

'You're a terrible liar, Ben Deacon.'

She listened to herself talking, an actress in a play which she was observing from the wings, script utterly remote from her own predestined scenario.

'Okay, so they were given to me by grateful patients. Did I say I bought them?'

She prepared some of the food and the actress on the stage ate with a healthy appetite, drank two glasses of claret.

Ben squeezed lemon on to a slice of smoked salmon. 'I know it's Christmas but I think you should know there have been developments.'

'Developments? What kind of developments?' the actress asked.

'I can't tell you right now.'

'The licence plate?'

'That and other leads.' His voice was grave. 'Which reminds me, the police want to see the Mauser.' He fetched it from the living-room and put it in his night bag.

'So why can't you tell me about the developments?' Her lines came to her easily.

'It wouldn't be fair if what I suspect isn't true. I'll tell you when the call comes – if I'm right.'

'Okay. Now, you'd better get some sleep.' She handed him a capsule.

'You don't seem too worried.'

True – she wasn't. She said: 'I often think about my grandfather on my father's side. He was a fine old man, a great fisherman. I can see him now sitting beside the water, rod and line part of him.'

'I don't see –'

'The point is it doesn't matter whether you're alive or dead. He's just as alive to me now as he was then. His beard smelled of snuff,' she added.

Ben frowned. 'I think you should get an early night, too.'

'Don't worry, I'm okay.' The actress kissed the actor and exited left.

She cleaned up in the kitchen and deliberated whether or not to take a sedative herself; she decided she would because, conscious, her detached vision might degenerate. She set the alarm clock for half an hour before dawn and placed it under the pillow on the bed so that, although it would wake her, its call wouldn't reach the spare room.

Before closing the curtains she gazed towards the forest, saw a red glow moving slowly through the birch trees. Every few seconds or so it burned brighter: small but not small enough to be a cigarette. A cigar. Havana illegally imported into Tampa.

She waved. The glow fell. Died abruptly. Squashed underfoot.

She drew the curtain and climbed into bed, it smelled of lavender and childhood.

She was awoken once by a scream. She ran to the spare room where Ben was sitting upright, sweat beading his face. 'A nightmare,' she said. 'Go back to sleep.' She wiped the sweat from his face, held him while he lowered himself to the pillow. 'Happy Christmas,' he said and closed his eyes. When his breathing had steadied she switched out the bedside lamp and went back to her room.

Chapter Twenty-Two

You will go to the lake to keep the pledge you made on another Christmas Day.

The muffled beep of the alarm clock is her heart beat. Sliding one hand under the pillow, she switches it off.

A shark fin of terrible certainty.

She steps out of bed and observes herself once more, notices in the bathroom mirror that the actress has been crying. She doesn't shower but washes her face with scrupulous intent so that it is quite naked. She dresses in her paint-spattered clothes.

She draws the curtains in the bedroom. Dawn has just reached the forest and laid fingers on the ground mist. She opens the window, hears voices calling her from the Indian burial ground.

Sidles into the spare room. Ben's face is contorted in the new light and his lips are moving, but he is still deeply asleep. She leaves the envelope containing her note to him on the bedside table beside the telephone extension.

Still observing herself in the play, she descends the stairs, taking care to avoid the step that creaks.

The horoscope has arrived early this festive morning. Just one line. She understands – the Christmas Day long ago when Harry proposed.

In the kitchen she is assailed by familiarity. She stretches and plucks a sprig of rosemary from the swatch hanging from the ceiling. It smells mauve.

She opens the door and steps into the dawn.

Halfway across the lawn she hears the phone ring in the house. It shatters her detachment as surely as a curtain bell in a theatre.

Whimpering, she breaks into a run.
Towards the forest.
The burial ground.
The lake.
Towards the final act.

He stood beside the alder on the spur above the lake: theatrical hat, spectacles glinting, granny scarf flapping. Hand beckoning.

She ran joyously.
Then he was gone.
She stopped on the spur, trampled grass at her feet beginning to unfold. She called out: 'Harry?'
Silence. Except for the faint creak of ice weakened by the thaw.
'Harry . . .'
A voice came from the end of the rotting jetty. 'I'm here, Sarah. Waiting.'
His voice.
She scrambled down the bank of the spur on to the jetty. 'I'm coming, Harry!'
'Hurry.'
She was near the end of the jetty when the boards beneath her feet snapped. One. Two. Three. As she fell she felt the protruding spikes of wood rip her clothes. Then she hit the ice.
Shouts from the shore.
A gunshot.
She hoisted herself into a crouch.
Another shot.
She stood up and took a step forward. As the ice opened around her.

Down. Water filling her lungs, weighting her. Rippling grey light in her eyes.
She tried to swim, but without resolution, because this was the way it had been written. She shouted: 'Harry!' and saw his name float away in a bubble.

Another suck of water into her lungs; cold lead. She grasped at the crust of ice and felt it break in her hand. Grasped one of the piles of the jetty, but her fingers couldn't grip the slimy surface.

Then she was under the ice. Staring through it the way Harry had stared, sightlessly. But there was a distorted face peering down at her. Like the face in the skylight.

A hammer blow. The skylight shattering . . . strong unblemished light in her eyes . . .

Then she heard Ben Deacon's authoritative voice. 'Don't die, Sarah. *Don't* die.'

She could hear his laboured breathing as he swam, then strode, through the jostling shards of ice, pulling her behind him.

They reached the shallows, then a narrow strip of gravel beach. He lifted her from the waist, head down, and she felt water pour from her throat. Then he laid her on her back, pinched her nostrils shut, placed his lips to her mouth and breathed into her: four quick breaths followed by a more measured rhythm. Her lungs expanded and contracted of their own accord. Taking his lips from her mouth, he helped her into a sitting position, back against the bank of the spur.

The Mauser lay on the gravel in front of her, beside a wooden mallet. A few yards away lay a body, blood staining the front of the Crombie topcoat, granny scarf covering the face, cracked spectacles protruding from beneath it.

Ben Deacon hooked one foot round the scarf and tugged. *The unveiling of a sculpture at an exhibition*, Sarah thought, as she stared at the marble-white face of Mike Kaplan.

Chapter Twenty-Three

All will be revealed . . .

Sarah's first visitor in the hospital near Holyfield where she had been taken for observation was Ben Deacon.

Pulling up a chair beside the bed in her private ward, he said: 'I thought you'd like to know you're not crazy.'

'Running along a jetty to meet a dead man isn't crazy?'

'You were suffering from an over-dose of Special K, the latest street drug. Ketamine Hydrochlorine. I should have guessed – it was used to treat traumas in Vietnam, but it's out of favour now because it can cause horrific hallucinations. It's related to Angel Dust and it's poised to take over from Ecstasy. Cheap too, maybe only ten dollars a hit.'

She stared at him uncomprehendingly.

'Special K was put in your sleeping capsules, leaving just enough phenobarbitol to make you sleep. The mix tore you apart – terrifying dreams followed by hallucinations. I should know: I took one on Christmas Eve.'

'To make me *think* I was crazy!'

'And to make you more amenable to any suggestions – commands, really – that your astrologer made. Ultimately you were so confused about fantasy and reality that you would have jumped off the Empire State if the stars had told you to.'

'I don't understand. Christmas Day . . . What happened?"

Taking her hand, as he used to when she was lying on his couch, Ben Deacon told her.

The phone rang beside the bed in the spare room. Fighting his way out of a nightmare, Ben stretched out a heavy arm and picked it up.

His receptionist. She was sorry about it being Christmas Day but he had told her to call him whatever, whenever. Anyway, as instructed, she had driven to the consulting rooms to check the fax – and there was the message he had been expecting from a private detective.

Ben shook off the shreds of the nightmare, listened intently. All his suspicions about the Society of Distressed Artists were true, according to the fax.

He thanked her – Ginger Rogers! – and promised her a raise.

The police had telephoned too, she said. They had traced the owner of the green car: an ex-con named Ryder who had served prison sentences for violence and extortion.

Replacing the receiver, he noticed the envelope; he opened it, read her note, checked her bedroom, struggled into a sweater and pants, ran down the stairs.

Windows ballooned, colours vibrated. He thought: 'Hell of a time to go down with a fever.' He checked the fax. *You will go to the lake* . . . He returned to the spare room, grabbed the Mauser from his night bag and ran rubber-legged towards the forest and the lake beyond.

On the sliver of beach stood a figure wearing a broad-brimmed hat, scarf, spectacles. He shouted and the figure turned, pointing a hand-gun.

He shot Mike Kaplan. Twice.

Sarah waited while a nurse snooped. When she had gone she said: 'But I heard Harry's voice.'

'On a cassette recorder. Kaplan slid it along the ice to the end of the jetty on a length of wire, so he could retrieve it. He knew you'd fall through the boards because he had cracked them with a mallet. If you'd made it to the shore . . .'

'He would have hit me with the mallet?'

'Probably. And tossed you off the jetty again. And it would have been assumed that you hit your head when you fell – on the jagged boards of the piles.'

'I still don't understand. Why would Mike want to kill me?'

'This is the worst part,' Ben said.

'Harry?'

'Is alive and well, living under an assumed name in San Francisco with a woman named Pauline Crossley. *Was* living,' he corrected himself. 'The cops raided Kaplan's apartment and found his address. He was arrested yesterday and made a full confession.'

Sarah bowed her head and examined her clenched hands.

'How much are you worth, Sarah?'

'About two and a half million dollars.'

'Some policy! Harry was very astute to take it out on *your* life. And to try to collect after *his* death.'

Sarah unclenched her hands and studied the marks her nails had left on the palms.

'He and Kaplan were up to their eyeballs in debt when they were running the gallery together,' Ben said. 'To pay off their creditors – and set up another gallery somewhere in Europe – they needed money. Yours.'

'But I left my money to the Society for Distressed Artists.'

'Who advised you to leave it to them?'

'Mike Kaplan,' Sarah said, covering her face with her hands.

'Hardly surprising. Mike *is* – *was* – the Society for Distressed Artists. All donations passed through his hands – into them, rather. And stayed there.'

'But I saw Harry's body,' Sarah said from between her hands.

Ben shook his head. 'You thought you saw Harry's body. Did you examine it closely?'

'The face wasn't . . . recognizable, the police said I needn't bother. They showed me his clothes, his credit cards, his cigar cutter even . . . Who was he?' Sarah asked.

'A vagrant Harry and Kaplan picked up on the Lower East Side someplace. Same height, same build as Harry. They knocked him unconscious, mutilated his face and threw him in the lake when it was freezing. All that stuff about a body surfacing after ten days – well, maybe it does but it stays under the ice just the same and when it's finally found . . .'

'The eels.'

Ben hurried on. 'But they couldn't just murder you because the police would have investigated and they might have discovered everything.'

'So they tried to scare me to death?'

'And make you and everyone else think you were crazy. But the first thing Harry had to do was disappear. To San Francisco.'

'With Pauline Crossley.'

'Then Kaplan took over, made your horoscopes come true so that you would believe them, obey them.'

'How could he do that?'

'Easy,' Ben said, 'if he had someone working with the astrologer.'

'The Puerto Rican girl?'

'She read the predictions before they were transmitted and told an accomplice, an ex-con named Ryder, who told Kaplan. The day the Peeping Tom looked through the sky-light . . . What was your prediction that day?'

'You will be subject to attentions from a stranger.'

'There you go! A cinch. Ryder peers through the sky-light, then vanishes. What about the day Harris was poisoned?'

'Be particularly protective with children or surrogates.'

'Simple. A call to Harry in San Francisco. 'Where does Harris run? In the forest? What part? Okay, Harry. Thanks, old buddy. See you in Paris, or Rome, or London.' And Kaplan, or Ryder, tosses poisoned meat in the forest.'

Sarah took her hands away from her face and frowned. 'But some of the horoscopes must have been fakes.' *Prepare yourself for a loss in the family* –the day Harry disappeared. *A long lost member of the family could return* – the day she found his body. The vagrant's body, that was.

'Sure, some were doctored when Carmen Barea transmitted them. But in the early days it was mostly your life that was manipulated. Harry gave Kaplan the keys to the house, the studio, the hot-house . . . Ryder slashed the nude, released the butterflies, smoked cigars, made the phone call from the studio, substituted the real Mauser for the replica – he was in the green car, he knew you'd bought one.'

'One day there wasn't a horoscope.'

'What day of the week?'

A Sunday, Sarah told him.

'The day Carmen Barea normally transmitted all the horoscopes. She omitted you deliberately, to send you into withdrawal – with the help of Special K. – and soften you up. Bad horoscopes, good ones: hot, cold, all part of the process.'

'And it worked,' Sarah said.

'Sometimes the predictions came true of their own accord, I have to admit that.'

'What about the deserted house?'

'Stage-managed. The climax was drawing near – by that time Kaplan had fitted himself out with clothes identical to Harry's – and *all* the horoscopes were phonies.'

'Harry's voice . . . another tape?'

'On the same cassette as the one Kaplan played at the lake.'

'Supposing I hadn't run along the jetty?'

'They pretty well knew you would. Don't forget Kaplan was observing your behaviour. But in any case, they would have got you one way or another. Think about it; the car smash – I'm willing to bet the brakes were fixed, the circular saw, the loaded Mauser . . . You *did* point the replica at your own head.'

'Bang,' Sarah said.

'One thing might have saved you: success. That was always a possibility.'

'You mean my paintings?'

'*Nude Slashed*, *Nude with a Gun* . . . They were hot. Could have made you and the gallery a lot of money.'

'Not two and a half million dollars!'

'Who knows? In any case you blew it, told Kaplan you weren't going to paint any more.'

'How did they know there would be ice on the lake on Christmas Day?'

'Ever look at the met reports on the television? They're usually accurate these days.'

'All of which leaves one hell of a question. Why did Rebecca Cotton do this to me?'

'Let her tell you,' Ben said.

He opened the door and Sarah's second visitor of the day walked in.

What do you say to someone you've been trying to frighten to death? Even though you didn't realize it?

Rebecca Cotton didn't know now any more than she did when she had left New York City earlier that day with Sarah's forecast. 'Five minutes,' she said. 'That's all I ask.'

'That's *all*?' Sarah hoisted herself higher on the pillows. 'Jesus Christ, it had better be good.'

Rebecca sat on a chair on the other side of the bed from Ben and began to talk.

The first ambiguous threat . . . the second, heightened by the knife in Ryder's hand . . . the kidnap . . . Carmen Barea's duplicity . . . the instructions to fix the horoscopes if she valued her son's life . . .

'You could have called the cops!'

'Every time I thought about it I saw the knife at Robbie's throat. And I didn't know they were trying to kill you.'

'What did you think they were doing, trying to persuade me to join a painting by numbers class?'

'They were my predictions too. Gemini, the twins . . . *"Dawn tomorrow is the time . . ."*'

'For what? You weren't going to drown, were you, Rebecca?'

'Christmas Day was when my fate was going to be settled. And Robbie's. And it was, wasn't it.'

'For me, sure. Why for you?'

Rebecca said to Ben: 'You tell her.'

Ben had driven Sarah to hospital, then returned to the house where he had read half a dozen of the horoscopes stacked beside Sarah's fax and called Rebecca Cotton.

'Mrs Cotton isn't here. She's spending Christmas in New Hampshire.' A girl's voice, Spanish accent.

'Give me her number – it's very urgent.'

'You're a client?'

'No.' He was visited by inspiration. 'I'm a cop and we're investigating an attempt to murder a woman named Sarah Logan.'

'*Madre mia*!' An intake of breath, 'If I help –'

'You'll be okay, I promise."

She told him about Robbie's abduction and gave him an address in the Bronx near the Yankee Stadium: the same address to which Ryder, the owner of the green car, had been traced.

'But go real careful,' the girl said. 'He's got the boy there.'

There was a shout, the sound of a scuffle and the line went dead. So Rebecca Cotton wasn't in New Hampshire . . .

He called the police and told them he believed Ryder was holding a boy hostage at the address in the Bronx.

They staked out the house, a tenement, and waited until Ryder emerged – to get cigarettes maybe, or a fix. No one ever knew because when he was challenged he started to run and they shot him dead.

They found a gun in his belt. A Mauser. A replica.

'I'm sorry about what I did,' Rebecca said to Sarah. 'I had no choice.'

'Tell me one thing: after I was dead, after you had got your boy back, would you have talked?'

Rebecca shook her head. 'Robbie's life would still have been threatened.'

'And Kaplan would have destroyed all the evidence,' Ben said. 'Phoney horoscopes, cassettes with Harry's voice on them . . .'

'Can I show you why I did what I did?' Rebecca said.

'Okay.'

Rebecca opened the door and Sarah's third visitor of the day walked in. Robbie.

After a few seconds Sarah said: 'I understand, I guess. Do you,' to Robbie, 'want to come back to the house when I get out of here later today?'

'Do you have a computer?' Robbie said.

'An Apple,' Sarah told him.

'Great. Because I'm on the point of hacking into the Kremlin.'

Chapter Twenty-Four

A time for change . . .

The first day of spring.

Rebecca Cotton, studying at the School of Visual Arts on West 21st Street, strolls around the gallery where Sarah Logan's exhibition has finally been staged after her acquittal on charges of obscenity.

She stops in front of *Nude Slashed*. One day, she thinks, I will exhibit here. Nudes.

As night falls Sarah Logan swallows the last of her tea, opens the kitchen door and walks across the lawn to the rebuilt studio.

On the way she points the beam of her flashlight into the hot-house. Wings, fragile and folded, quiver; the false eyes of *Attacus atlas* peer at her, ephemerally defiant.

In the studio Sarah stares at an empty canvas and decides that it should stay that way because, sensationalism apart, she does not possess original talent.

But if Rebecca Cotton can abandon the stars and take up painting why cannot she do the same in reverse – in an amateur role? After all, they are heavenly twins.

She picks up a book she has bought in New York and makes her first tentative incursion into astrology. Her subject: Rebecca Cotton – and thus herself as well. *You will be subject to attentions from a stranger* . . .

She shivers and tries again. . . . *attentions from someone who has been estranged too long.* Better. Will Cotton? Ben Deacon?

She pauses and glances at the sky-light. The stars, glimmering, return her gaze.